TWO BONE
ANTHOLOGY 2

TWO BONE ANTHOLOGY 2

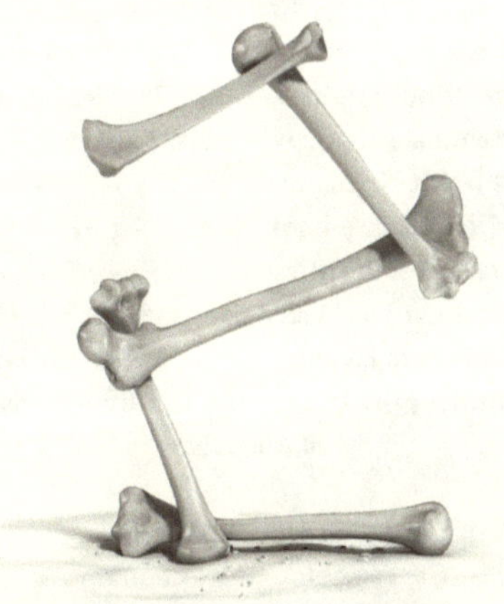

T.K. WRATHBONE

☠ Royal Star Publishing ☠

Skull & Bone is an imprint of Royal Star Publishing
www.royalstarpublishing.com.au

Previously released as a paperback in 2017, this edition published 2018
All Rights Reserved, Copyright ©T.K. Wrathbone 2017, 2018

Trade Paperback ISBN: 978-1-925683-81-3
Large Print Paperback ISBN: 978-1-922307-03-3
Case Laminate Hardcover ISBN: 978-1-922307-04-0
Dust Jacket Hardcover ISBN: 978-1-922307-05-7
The Orphanage e-book ISBN: 978-1-925683-25-7
Hantel & Gresel: Food Critics e-book ISBN: 978-1-925683-27-1
Mirror, Mirror On The Wall e-book ISBN: 978-1-925683-29-5
The Bones Of Wrath: Haunted e-book ISBN: 978-1-925683-31-8
A catalogue record for this book is available from the National Library
of Australia.

Cover design: Royal Star Publishing and Odyssey Books
Cover photos: istock.com/koya79
Typesetting in Minion Pro by Royal Star Publishing

CONTENTS

THE ORPHANAGE

CHAPTER ONE

Penelope stood before the old battered steps that led to the old battered door. Her eyes moved up to the imposing windows of the three-storey battered old building that stood before her. It was cold, grey, and dismal.

The butterflies in her stomach stopped playing nice and became competing dragons, wreaking havoc by getting revenge on each other in a sick game of tag.

She was going to *be* sick.

Her hand flew to her mouth and she tried not to retch, but doubled over briefly, gasping for air, waiting for the feeling to pass.

"Come along, dear," the social worker said from behind her. "It's going to be your home now."

Penelope slowly rose, her gaze moved back up, and she now saw a curious face in the window… staring down…at her…

I don't want to be here, she vehemently thought, gripping the handle of her bag until her knuckles turned white. *Why should I have to be here?*

Mrs Grey, the social worker, waved her up the stairs. She was already standing on the porch talking to a man.

Penelope stood rooted to the spot. She glanced around at the forbidding demeanour of the building. Ragged bushes ran along the wall, ivy climbed upward making its way into every crack and crevice. Bubbling white paint was chipping or missing.

The landscape wasn't much better, just barren wasteland with a few trees dotted amongst it.

Her gaze landed back on Mrs Grey, and with fear in her heart, she removed one hand from her bag to grasp the handle of her suitcase, which she ever so slowly rolled over the pale grey gravel and up the battered, chipped stone steps toward the door.

"Penelope, this is the headmaster, Dr Livè. He will be taking you from here. Doctor, this is Penelope Black, you already have her papers so I'll leave her with you."

"Thank you, Mrs Grey," the tall stony faced man said. He had a nose like a beak, and his face was long and thin just like the rest of him. He clasped his long thin fingers in front of him. "Come along, Penelope, we have a bed waiting for you." He stepped inside and held the door open for her.

Mrs Grey laid a hand on Penelope's shoulder as she passed, but moved on without a word.

Penelope watched the social worker get in her car and drive away before turning her head back to the headmaster who was impatiently waiting for her. It was all in slow motion, like some kind of movie.

"Come along, Miss Black," Dr Livè spat between clenched teeth. "I don't have *time* for you to waste."

Penelope heaved a sigh and rolled her lonely little blue suitcase through the imposing doorway into an even more battered foyer. Cold grey stone blocks for a floor, old wood panels for walls, and everything was bare. No rugs, no paintings, no furniture.

Penelope glanced down each hallway as they passed. All were bare and sadly lacking in anything other than coldness. She followed Livè upstairs and down hallways until they were standing in a six bed room.

"The last one on the right is yours." Livè stood with his hands behind his back. His cold demeanour matched the building.

They're perfectly suited, Penelope thought as she rolled towards the bed.

"You store your case under the bed, your clothes in the cupboard beside you. The bathroom is down the hallway. Breakfast is at eight, lunch at one, and dinner at six. There is no eating in-between, all rules must be followed, and classes are from nine until one and two until five. Just because you are here does not mean you will cease studies. They are the backbone of Kingsmere Orphanage." He turned on his heel and walked for the door. "The bell is about to go, you can start classes after lunch."

Penelope watched his retreating back until it had left the room then checked her watch. Twelve-thirty, half an hour till lunch. She sat on the bed, put her head in her hands and sobbed.

She sobbed for the months of heartache at the pain of losing her parents. She sobbed for the fear of having nowhere to go until social services dumped her in an orphanage. She sobbed at the fear of how many years she would have to be in this hell hole.

"It's like that for all of us when we come here."

Penelope's head shot up, and through a million tears saw a white girl about her age in a school uniform standing in front of her holding out a box of tissues. She quickly wiped her face.

"Here," the girl said, holding the box closer.

Penelope grabbed a couple and wiped up the mess she must have been.

The girl sat down. "All of us have done that the day we come here. I've seen them come and go and yet everyone cries their first day." She swung her long brown braid over her shoulder. "I'm Alexandra, but everyone calls me Alex. I'm fourteen and have been here for five years."

Penelope stared at her. "You've been *here* for *five years*…since…you were nine…how…I mean…how have you survived it?"

Alex shrugged. "I just did. You just have to. Your parents are gone and no one else wants you, so you just *have* to survive."

Penelope gasped back some air. "I don't know what to do… I've never been in an orphanage before." Tears streamed down her face once more and she grabbed more tissues from the box.

Alex gave her a supportive smile. "None of us have. But we just have to get used to it, and deal with it, and make the best of what we got. Which is a roof over our heads, three meals a day, a bed at night and schooling, so when we leave we'll be able to go to college or Uni or just get a job."

Penelope stared out of the window at the gloomy sky. She felt just as gloomy on the inside.

"What's your name?"

She glanced at Alex and shrugged. "Penelope. But everyone calls me Penny."

"And how old are you?"

"Thirteen."

"That's good," Alex said. "You're the same age as us. We're all in this room, there's a room for the thirteen, fourteen and fifteen year olds, and then the sixteen and seventeen year olds have rooms of their own. The same with the younger kids. You'll fit in with us."

That wasn't really much consolation for Penny, who stood up and opened the tiny slim cupboard beside the bed. There was hanging space and one shelf.

"It's not much, but we don't come here with much," Alex said. "Do you want help? The lunch bell's going to ring any minute."

Penny turned. "Um, do you mind?"

Alex shook her head. "Not at all."

They quickly opened Penny's case and hung up some of her clothes as not all would fit. She had artfully arranged everything in her case so she could take as much of it as possible, so most of it was left in the case which was tucked away under the bed. She changed into the uniform that was laid out neatly on the end of the bed, and placed a small silver frame with a picture of her and her parents on the small bedside cupboard.

"We all have one of them," Alex said wistfully.

Penny glanced around at the other beds and saw frames on each nightstand.

"When did they…?"

"Four months ago…"

"…I'm sorry…"

"…Me too…"

The bell rang for lunch.

"Time to go, come on, you can sit with us." Alex ran for the door.

"Us?" Penny asked, following Alex out the door. She saw Alex was already down the hallway. Penny ran to keep up and trailed after her as she ran down the stairs, along the hall, and stopped at the doorway. Penny was caught in a jumble of other kids, but made her way to Alex's side.

"There you are," Alex said. "The boys aren't here yet, but we'll get a table."

"Boys?" Penny followed Alex to a table.

"Yep, we have boys and girls here," Alex replied, waving someone over.

Penny turned to see three boys walking their way over and froze. *What am I supposed to do with boys?* she thought as they approached.

"Everyone, this is Penny, she's new today," Alex introduced her. "Penny, the tall one is Adrian, and the twins are Alistair and Alfred."

"Hello," all four said at once.

"I'm starving Al, what about you?" Adrian asked.

"Absolutely," Alistair, Alfred and Alex all said at the same time.

Penny giggled slightly, her hand over her mouth to hold it back.

"What's so funny?" Alex asked as they headed for the food line.

"You all answered when he said Al," Penny whispered.

"That's coz when you shorten our names they're all Al," Alex whispered back and grabbed a food tray.

Moving past the food ladies, they had slop after slop dumped on their plates.

Penny wrinkled her nose as they walked back to their table. "What *is* this?"

"Don't worry," Alex said. "It actually tastes better than it looks."

Penny took a seat next to her and watched as the others dug in. Looking down at her meal, she thought it looked awful, but smelt rather good. They had bread rolls, potato, vegetables, and some sort of meat thing in fluid. She picked up her fork and sampled some of it. It tasted okay. Making her way through her meal she watched the other kids. All were orphans just like her. No parents, no family, nobody to take care of them. Tears welled up and she quickly blinked them away, glad her table mates were so busy with their food that they hadn't noticed.

"Oh, my God, there's Stacey. Look at her. Just

like all the others." Alex stared at the doorway.

Everyone in the room had stopped worrying about their food to stare at the girl who had entered the lunch room.

She looked awful. Her skin was grey, her cheeks sunken, her eyes hollow. She looked ill. She looked out of it.

Adrian sighed. "That's *how many* now?"

"Ten," Alistair and Alfred replied together.

Penny looked at them. "Ten what?"

"Ten kids that have been off sick for a few days, only to come back looking worse than when they left," Alex said.

They all watched the young girl wander in a daze over to the food line and gather her meal. But then she just stood there looking at everyone, as though she had no clue as to what to do next.

A girl got up and helped her to their table where she sat and started eating.

They all watched for a few moments more before going back to their own meals.

"So why is ten kids getting sick a big deal? It *is* winter," Penny said, smoothing her roll with the remains of her food.

The boys stopped eating to stare at her and she stopped to stare back, not sure if she had said anything wrong. "What?" she quietly asked.

"Penny doesn't know, guys," Alex reminded them before she started the story. "Over the past ten months, one kid per month has mysteriously been struck down with some illness. Now, the kid looks perfectly all right and is in school with the rest of us, but then boom, they're gone overnight. Sometimes, they'll come back a few days later, the same day another kid is mysteriously taken ill, and twice, the kids didn't come back at all." She nodded in Stacey's direction. "Stacey is number ten. So, it's not just because it's winter and we might be getting normal colds and flus. It's been happening for ten months now."

Penny studied Stacey's face and body language. The poor girl could barely feed herself. "So there was nothing wrong with her and now there is?"

Alex looked at her. "Exactly. Look at her; she looks worse than when she supposedly became sick."

She really didn't look good, but the ugly grey woollen uniform dress she had on didn't help.

They finished off their meal just before the bell rang.

"We've got five minutes to get to class," Alex said and they all got up to put their empty trays onto the trolley for clearing.

"Okay, so here's how classes work," Alex said as she led Penny to their classroom. "Boys are separated from girls, and girls are separated into age groups. Six to twelves and thirteens to seventeens. We all stay in the same classroom and the teachers go around instead of us, so there ain't a hundred kids moving in the corridors all the time. We have two classes a day, five days a week and each one is different. We don't get homework, just revision or reading as we do most of it in class." She walked into a room with ten rows of desks, five rows across. The walls and floor was like everywhere else, cold and barren. The old-fashioned desks and chairs were hard plastic. The bell rang for everyone to be in their seats and a woman walked in the door.

"Be seated," she proclaimed and proceeded with maths class.

"Ah, miss," Alex called out with her arms raised.

The woman looked up in annoyance. "You don't interrupt…" She noticed Alex pointing to Penny. "Oh, a new one…you'll need books." She rummaged around in a cupboard. "Come and get them."

Alex waved a scared Penny up as she looked around in confusion.

After Penny slowly made her way to the front of the room the teacher threw a fifth book onto the pile she'd been making and then dumped them all into Penny's arms.

"And your name is?" she asked.

"P…P…Penny," she muttered.

"Well, Penny, place your name on the inside of the books in pencil and they can stay in your desk for the remainder of the time you're with us. Now, take your seat."

Penny hastily moved back to her desk which was beside Alex's and took the pencil she offered. It took all of her brain power to keep up with what was being taught. She hadn't gotten this far in her old school and had then been out for four months. Now she was learning about things she'd never heard of, and it was all rather confusing. And three hours later she was still confused.

"Phew," she said, shaking her head. "That was a bit too much for my brain to take in. I hadn't done anything like that in my old school."

"It'll take a few weeks to get used to it all, but come on, let's freshen up," Alex said.

Penny followed Alex upstairs to their floor and made their way into the bathroom.

"This is where we shower. It's for everyone on this floor so we all share. The toilets are that way." Alex pointed left. "And the showers that way." She pointed right. "Five of each, so it can get a bit crowded."

"And it's not like we need the time or space to make ourselves beautiful," a thin blonde girl said. "I'm Melanie, and you're new."

"Um, yeah," Penny said. "Today."

"I think we're sharing a room," Melanie went on. "With Sasha, Rachael and Michelle." She pointed to each girl who waved in return.

Alex came out of the toilet stall. "That's Penny," she said before Penny could open her mouth again. "She's thirteen and has awesome clothes."

Penny's slight smile disappeared. "Are we not supposed to have nice clothes in here?"

Rachael spoke up. "Not all of us get to keep what we come in with. Not all of us had nice stuff beforehand. Best be careful, some might go missing." She washed her hands and smoothed her neat ponytail.

"M-missing," Penny stuttered. "I-I, don't want to lose anything, they're the last things my mother bought for me. Most of it was thrown out when the house was cleared out." She saddened. "Most of what *I had* got thrown out and that's all the social worker allowed me to take." The thought of losing so much a second and third time was too much for Penny who burst into tears.

"There, there." Alex patted her back as more girls came in. "Let's go back to our room." She led Penny back to their room while the others piled in. "It's still so new and fresh for you." She helped Penny sit on her bed and rubbed her back. "It gets easier after a year or two."

That made Penny cry even harder and the girls crowded round.

"I wasn't allowed to bring anything," Sasha said. "They just took me into social services and then dropped me here. They had to buy me stuff, clothes and toiletries and a bag. All I have is one photo of my family."

"I had a few things and was lucky enough to take them the day they took me," Rachael added.

"We've all lost a lot," Melanie added. "I've been here two and a half years. It doesn't get easier."

"And they don't let you buy anything," Sasha added. "They give you generic soap and shampoo and stuff."

Penny wiped her face. "You said it might go missing; have you all had things stolen? I don't want to lose the only things I have left from my parents."

"Some of the boys have lost stuff," Alex said, then pulled a face. "But they probably lose it themselves because, well, they're boys."

The girls laughed.

"And a couple of girls have said stuff has gone missing, but then it's turned up so…" Melanie shrugged. "Not sure what really happens."

"It's best to keep your best stuff locked in your case which you did before," Alex told Penny. "Don't tell anyone the combo of that case and change it often."

"It's not like we're allowed nice stuff anyways." Rachael picked at the ugly grey dress she was wearing. "We all wear the same uniform five days a week, and we're not allowed to go anywhere on the weekend, or after school. Unless it's our once a month trip into town."

"And we all have to wash these hideous things," Sasha said, pulling up her grey socks. "We all get set nights to go down and do our washing in the basement laundry."

"It's just one of the skills they claim we'll need for life out in the real world," Alex said. "Which I guess is true."

"My mum was teaching me how to wash when she…" Tears welled in Penny's eyes and rolled down her cheek as her lip quivered.

Alex squeezed her hand. "We've all lost a mum, so we know what it's like. Just hang on to the memories and what she taught you."

"That's what we all have to do," Melanie added quietly. "We all have to."

The dinner bell rang and they found themselves in line behind Stacey.

"Hey, Stace, how are you?" Alex asked, giving her a slight nudge to move forward.

The girl turned, looking sicker than at lunchtime. "Fine," she mumbled, staring straight through them.

Alex nodded slowly. "Riiiggght, um, this is Penny. She's new today."

Stacey's gaze never changed. "Hello."

"Hello," Penny replied, wondering if Stacey was on drugs.

Alex nudged Stacey along the line. "So, what are you sick with then?"

Stacey stared down at the food on her tray. "I'm not sick."

Alex and Penny exchanged glances. "Um, of course you're sick, Stace. Your skin is grey, your eyes sunken, cheeks hollow. Definitely not healthy like before."

Stacey came to the end of the line. "I'm fine. Better than before."

Alex and Penny stood there for a moment pondering Stacey's condition.

"Come on, get a move on." Adrian gave them a shove from behind and they all hurried over to their table.

"Man, did you see Stacey up close," Alex furiously whispered. "Even sicker looking than from afar."

"Some of the boys were like that when they came back," Adrian mumbled between bites. "Looked far worse than what they'd been, and they all appeared drugged. Like they'd been infected with something."

"Zombies!" Alistair piped up. "They were like

zombies with mummified brains. Couldn't think, couldn't talk, looked half dead." He nodded confidently. "Zombies."

Alfred snorted in laughter. "Couldn't be anything else."

Adrian rolled his eyes. "You two and your supernatural theories." He looked around to see if anyone else was listening. "I've heard rumours and whispers, and add them to the weird stuff going on in the middle of the night. Something's definitely going on. I have to wonder if we're being used as guinea pigs."

"Guinea pigs for what?" Alex asked.

"Drug experiments." Adrian nodded authoritatively.

"Ooh, like drugs that make you a zombie?" Alfred asked. "Ughhhh…brains…"

"Knock it off," Adrian snapped. "Real stuff is happening to the kids here at Kingsmere. Maybe big drug companies are trialling their drugs on us kids. We have no parents or guardians to say no, the headmaster would be giving permission, and is probably being given a hefty lump of money for it. How do you think he drives that red Ferrari?" He shovelled a forkful of mashed potato into his mouth. "Mmm?"

Penny sat enthralled, looking back and forth from the twins to Adrian to Alex. Conspiracies, zombies, evil drug companies. What a storm to walk into.

"So, they've been taking one kid a month to trial new drugs on?" Alex finished off her dessert.

"Rumour has it," Adrian said, pushing his tray

away and leaning his chin on his hand. "Don't know that it's true. But what else would make them look like that?" He flicked his thumb over his shoulder in the direction of Stacey. "And not all of the kids have returned to normal. Two of them didn't come back at all."

"And the rest of them never fully recovered from whatever was done to them," Alfred added to the conversation. "They've all been a bit…" He whistled and twirled his finger in circles at his temple. "Cuckoo."

"What better place to trial drugs than at an orphanage?" Adrian said.

The bell rang.

"What's that for?" Penny asked.

"To signify the end of dinner," Alex said. "Come on." Walking out of the dining hall, Alex informed Penny. "Dinner ends at seven, so we have a few hours before bedtime." They started up the stairs to their room. "The youngsters go to bed at eight when the bell rings. We go at nine, and the older kids go at ten. We all get about half an hour to get ready, finish up, and get to our rooms. I normally wait until the bell rings before getting ready for bed. The extra half hour helps."

They arrived at their room. "So normally we do a bit of reading or drawing for the next two hours. We don't get TV, radio, or internet, but there is a pool table in the rec room that you can convert into ping pong and other things. We also get different nights to do our washing. Ours is at the end of the week. So…" Alex jumped on her bed, "what do you want to do?"

A couple of other girls came in to collect some things.

Penny shrugged. "I don't know. I've never been in an orphanage before."

"Mmm, well then, I should take you on a tour, come on." Alex pulled Penny back out of the room and pointed down the hall to their right. "You know the bathroom's down that way, and so are the older girls' rooms. Below us on the next floor are the younger girls' rooms." They stopped at the balustrade and peered across the void in the staircase. "And across the way on that side are all the boys' rooms, our ages; the youngsters are on the floor below them." They moved down the stairs. "The floor above is where the teachers live, so don't ever go up there unless it's an emergency and you need help."

They made their way back to the ground floor. "There are five large classrooms, four for us, and one extra for other things. Library, staffroom, sickroom, main office, headmaster's office." They walked down hallway after hallway, left, right, all the same. Grey concrete block floors and wood walls. Bare. Cold. Empty.

"Here's the rec room." They stopped in the double doorway of a rather long narrow room. A pool table was at one end, with a dart board and a few chairs at the other. "It's not much, but the table converts, so that's helpful." They moved on. "There's a huge building outside with sporting equipment.

There was a pool, but they shut it down for winter. We have an oval for sport, and down in the basement…" She pushed open a door with basement clearly written on it. "Is the laundry room."

They stopped to see a group of kids unloading or loading the washers and dryers. "You have to do it all yourself. Our night is Friday night."

They walked down the darkly lit basement hall and Alex lowered her voice. "The super's office is here, as well as a storage area, but that doorway at the very end of the hall is off limits."

"Why?" Penny stared at the ominous door several feet in front of them.

Alex shrugged. "Don't know, and there's nothing written on the door. It's always locked, and if you're caught going in, or trying to, you get into trouble." She kept her voice low. "Some of the kids have said they hear weird noises coming from behind the door when they're down here doing laundry."

"What kind of noises?" Penny whispered, looking around to see if anyone was listening.

"Screams, bangs, machines going. Come on, let's go up, it's creeping me out."

They made it back up as the eight o'clock bell rang. "Time for the youngsters to get to bed." They watched a group head for the stairs. "They'll get the bathrooms now, and we'll get them in an hour. So, what do you want to do?"

Penny shrugged. "I dunno. If I were home I'd…" The thought trailed off, but still bought tears to her eyes.

"I know." Alex put her hand on Penny's shoulder. "We've all been there. The only thing to do now is pretend you're at boarding school and that we're your family."

Penny wiped away the tears. "Boarding school?"

Alex shrugged. "It's the only thing that keeps us all going. Pretending our parents all sent us to boarding school until we're eighteen." She became melancholic. "It's the only way to get through the loneliness. Come on, I'll show you the library." She linked her arm through Penny's and pulled her along. "It's not bad, full of good old literature and educational prose and what not. But there's no romance novels, no teen or young adult, or Jackie Collins," she said. "I think we've all read every book in here." They stopped in the abundantly filled library room with floor-to-ceiling shelves full of old texts, thesauruses and encyclopaedias.

"The Funk & Wagnalls are very good." Alex led Penny around the room. "And we've all used the poor encyclos for history and English to the point they're falling apart."

"How come we don't get homework?" Penny gazed at the ratty old furniture consisting of several worn out couches, single chairs, and a coffee table which had all had seen better days.

"The classes are three hours long, so everything we need to do we do it in those three hours, no need for homework. Except for English; sometimes we have to do some extra reading and stuff."

The bell rang.

"That's us," Alex said and pulled Penny along. "We have half an hour to get into bed, and trying to get around twenty other girls our age is near on impossible, so we take turns. Come on." Racing for the stairs, they collected their toiletries and made it into the bathroom to find other girls lining up.

"Bugger, we have to wait." Alex eyed off the shower stalls. "To make it easier and quicker, two rooms take their showers at night, the other two in the mornings. We're morning, is that all right?"

"Mmm, yeah, that's fine," Penny replied as they inched up the line, and moments later they were in the cubicles, then after taking ten minutes to brush their teeth and wash their faces, they made it back to their room in time to change for bed.

"Do we set alarms, or are we woken up?" Penny asked, reaching for her small alarm clock.

"We get woken up at seven by the bell," Melanie replied from her own bed next to Penny's. "We all get up at seven and breakfast is at eight."

Penny nodded. "That's what Dr Livè said."

"He's a weird one, isn't he?" Sasha pulled on her nightgown. Her bed was next to Alex's which was opposite Penny's. "I always found him to be cold."

"Uncaring."

"Unfeeling."

"Straight out weird," Alex finished off.

Penny nodded. "Is it true what Adrian said, that he drives a red Ferrari?"

Rachael snorted as she got into bed. "Thinks he's bloomin' Magnum PI the way he drives around."

"Meanwhile, we all go without any luxuries except what we're allowed to buy when we go into town."

Penny's eyes lit up. "We get to go shopping?"

"Well…" Melanie started.

"It's hardly shopping," Sasha finished.

"We're allowed to buy the 'female necessities'." Alex made quote marks with her fingers. "And the odd bit of junk food, but we're not allowed to bring anything back that's not necessary to our stay here."

Penny sighed. "So no music, magazines, clothes…?"

"Nope," came five replies.

"Girls, time for bed," the voice called down the hallway.

"That's the maths teacher from today. They do double duty and make sure we do as we're told."

The girls got into bed and Penny gazed wistfully at the photo of her and her parents. Emotions threatened to choke her, suffocate her, make her burst into tears.

"Think of it as boarding school," Alex called out. "It's the only way to stop all the emotions from killing you."

The other girls nodded in agreement.

"Lights out," the teacher called, and one by one each girl in each room flicked off her bedside light until darkness rained down. Until there was no light at all. And in the empty lonely isolation, Penny buried her head into her pillow and silently wept hot tears of pain. She knew her parent's death was an accident. They hadn't left her, or abandoned her on purpose. But it didn't stop the pain she felt. The pain she would probably feel for an eternity.

"Aaahhhhhhh…"

Penny struggled to wake.

"Aaahhhhhhh…"

Her eyelids were sluggish and fat and full of grit.

"Is that someone screaming?"

"What was that?"

"Aaahhhhhhh…"

Lights started popping on, and Penny raised her head to see some of the girls sitting up.

Alex pushed back her covers and swiftly made her way over to the window.

"Aaahhhhhhh…"

"There's lights on the oval," she said excitedly. "Look."

The rest of the girls climbed out of bed and moved to Alex's side. She was pointing to the small yellow balls of light bobbing in the distance.

"What is it?"

"What are they?"

"Are they ghosts?"

"They'll see us," Penny said. "We shouldn't have the lights on."

"Aaahhhhhhh…"

"Quick, turn the lights off," Alex gasped and Rachael and Michelle dashed around turning them off. They all blinked a few times and stared harder.

The lights were now bobbing over to the sports building off the side of the oval. They hovered at the front and then disappeared inside.

"It's probably the groundskeeper," Penny said

and then frowned. "Do you have a groundskeeper?"

"We do," Sasha said. "A weird duck who's also the super. He pulls double duty and does everything. Fixes the heating and cooling systems, mows the lawn."

"Hasn't painted the buildings in years though. They need a good paint," Rachael said. "He lurks a lot. Every time you turn around he's there."

They watched for a few more minutes, but saw and heard no more, so got back into bed.

"It's midnight." Alex checked her small clock. "It always happens at midnight."

"What does?" Penny asked, tucking the covers under her chin.

"A kid is always taken at midnight."

"How do you know?"

Alex shrugged. "Well, I don't know for sure, but other kids who bunk with the ones that become sick are woken by them being taken. Some have checked their clocks. Many say it happens at midnight. So we'll soon see if another kid has taken ill or not tomorrow."

The final light flicked out and the girls went back to sleep.

CHAPTER TWO

The next morning, the alarm went off at seven.

"Mmm." Penny snuggled down deeper into her bed. Her head ached and her eyes were gritty.

"Time to get up," a yawning Alex shook her.

Penny opened one eye.

"It's our turn in the showers. Come on."

Ever so reluctantly, Penny slowly climbed out of the bed and slid her feet into her slippers. She saw the other girls doing the same and grabbed her toiletry bag and dressing gown.

With only five showers between twenty-four girls, they washed their faces and brushed their teeth while waiting. After showering and getting dressed back in their room, the girls were finishing up with their hair when the breakfast bell rang.

"Okay," Alex said, looking in her cupboard. "Let's see who's missing."

Piling down to the dining room, Penny and Alex found the boys already at their table, and after taking a good look around the room, they went to stand in line.

"The girls are all here," Alex said. "What about the boys? Did you hear the screaming last night?"

"We heard," Adrian, Alistair and Alfred answered at the same time

"Any boys missing?"

"Mikey G isn't here," Adrian said softly.

They all looked around the room, not that Penny knew who Mikey G was.

And Alex wasn't even sure what he looked like. "Are you sure he's been taken," she asked. "In the middle of the night, at midnight?"

"Can't be sure," Adrian replied. "But after those screams last night, he's not here. And he can't *not* be here for any other reason."

"True." Alex nodded.

Penny was curious. "Why? Why not for any other reason?"

"None of us is ever adopted," Alex told her. "And we're only allowed to go into town once a month with a teacher, so there's no other reason for one of us not to be here."

"No one's ever adopted?" Penny asked, saddened by the thought of being in an orphanage for another five years.

"Not while I've been here," Alex said.

The bell rang for class, and after dumping their trays, they headed off to English.

Three hours later they were sitting on the back steps looking at the oval.

"What are we doing?" Penny asked, wrapping her coat around her against the cold winter breeze.

"We should be having lunch."

"Watching," Alex replied, looking through a small pair of binoculars at the oval.

"See anything?" Adrian walked up behind them and sat beside Penny, who froze at having a boy sitting beside her.

"Not really," Alex said. "But we should go for a better look."

The twins joined them as they started towards the oval.

"And where are you all going?" a man's voice boomed behind them.

They turned around.

"Going to walk the oval a couple of times," Adrian said, speaking to a man Penny hadn't seen before.

"What for?" the man called from the back porch.

"Exercise," Adrian replied simply.

"Hmph, very well then." The man stepped back inside.

"Who was that?" Penny asked as they turned and set off.

"The science teacher," Alfred replied. "Mr Humphreys."

"We get him tomorrow," Alex said as they tramped down the small incline and continued on to the oval.

"Okay," Adrian said when they got there. "Where were the lights?"

Alex turned to check the position of their room to the spot on the oval. "About there." She pointed to the middle of the oval.

They trekked over to the spot and started looking for clues. There was a light sprinkling of snow, not enough to completely blanket the grass, so they were able to see several drops of red stuff. They knelt down.

"That looks like blood," Alfred said, putting his face up close to the spots. "Red, round, drops." He stood up. "Definitely blood."

"So…?" Penny asked.

"So someone was out here and got clobbered," Adrian said. "Do they go towards the sports building?" He searched for drops and found some leading in the direction.

They followed the trail of drops to the sports building and saw they stopped at the door. They tried the handle, but it didn't open. They all plastered their faces against the window, but didn't see anything inside.

Adrian looked at his watch. "We've got time, let's go around the building and then head in."

They circled the sports building and pool hall looking for more blood, broken doors, windows, and items of clothing, anything that might indicate someone had been there or something had happened. But except for the blood on the oval, there was nothing.

Crunching across the light dusting of snow, they made it to the dining hall with half an hour to spare.

Inhaling burgers and fries, they thought about what it could mean. Had Mikey G been outside? Had he been caught? Hit over the head or worse, killed?

"Not enough blood," Alistair said.

"What?" Adrian asked.

"There was not enough blood for serious damage if it was Mikey G. Maybe a hit over the head? We didn't hear a gun or anything, so maybe he got hit. It was a steady flow of drops, nothing more."

"If it *was* Mikey G," Alfred said. "It could have been an animal or bird or something."

"So then where's Mikey G?" Adrian asked, polishing off his meal. "The kids in his room were told he was sick. But where is he and what happened?"

"Is it contagious?" Alistair replied. "The zombie flu strikes again!"

"It's nothing to do with zombies," Adrian chastised roughly. "So get it out of your head. We'll just have to wait to see if Mikey G comes back."

CHAPTER THREE

Friday after dinner, Alex took Penny down to the basement to do their washing. "We get about half hour each," she said. "We do our clothes then our bed linen, so two loads, then use the dryer, about fifteen minutes each. That way we all get a go since there's only five of each."

While waiting for their turn at the washers, they sat chatting about the week.

"So, how was your first week?" Alex asked as she filed her nails.

Penny looked down at her own nails. "Weird," she finally said with a shake of her head. "Not somewhere I ever thought I'd be."

"Yeah well, we all think that." Alex buffed the tops of her nails.

Penny shrugged. "I guess it helps thinking of it as a boarding school."

"It didn't stop you crying every night."

Penny shot a glance at Alex. "What makes you say that?"

Alex looked back. "Your eyes were red and puffy

every morning. It will get better and you'll only cry once a month or so."

Penny looked alarmed. "I'm going to forget my parents?"

Alex laughed softly. "No, that's not what I said, or meant. I meant you'll only cry at losing them and being here once a month."

A loud clanging made them turn toward the door.

"What was that?"

"Dunno, let's find out." Alex was on her feet and in the hallway in seconds with Penny right behind her.

Metal upon metal clanged again, and this time they definitely knew it was coming from the door at the end of the hall.

"What's going on?" Adrian, Alistair and Alfred came up behind them. "We were passing when we heard the sounds."

A few of the other students joined them, and they all stood looking as the door they were not allowed to go near stayed shut on whatever was making the noise.

A light flickered behind the glass panel in the door. It was red. Blood-red. And as the clanging continued, the kids inched closer and closer to the door.

"Aaahhh…"

"…Was that…?"

"Oh, my God…"

"What was that?" all whispered around the group.

"Maybe we should…" Penny started before Adrian strode toward the door and reached out his hand to grasp the handle. But he froze at the footsteps thumping toward him from the other side.

The door flew open, and Adrian and everyone else stepped back in surprise as the imposing figure stood in the doorway.

"What do you want? You know you're not supposed to come near this room." The great hulking figure of the groundskeeper-cum-super stood before them.

"We h-heard the noise," Adrian stuttered.

"Yeah well," the man said. "Just fixing the pipes, nothing to worry about, go back to what you were doing."

None of the kids moved.

"Go," he bellowed, and they all went scurrying back to their original activities.

Alex and Penny peeked around the laundry door, watching the super go back inside and lock the door.

"What's going on here?" Penny asked. "Everyone's weird."

Alex glanced at her. "Everyone? I hope you don't mean me?"

"No." Penny frowned. "I meant the staff. They're all weird."

"Mmm," Alex mumbled, going back to her basket of washing. "They can be. Like there's some big secret going on. The headmaster is definitely the ringleader. And I think the groundskeeper is his cohort."

"He does seem to do everything the headmaster tells him," Rachael said from her place in line behind the girls.

"And some of the teachers always steer clear of any questions you might ask them," Michelle added.

Alex and Penny finally got their turn at the washers and loaded up.

"But what's the big secret?" Alex asked, switching her machine on. "Why tell us to stay away from that door in the first place? They've just made us curious where we didn't care before."

"The quickest way to draw attention to something is to point it out and then tell people to stay away from it," Melanie said. "Now we notice it every time we're down here."

"But what's the big deal about it?" Matilda, a girl from another room, said. She had been folding her things into her basket whilst listening to the conversation going on. "If it's just a boiler room or something, then we're not going to go in there. It doesn't interest us or have anything to do with us."

"That's true." Sasha pulled the last of her things from the dryer. "But still, why draw attention to it in the first place?"

*****

On Saturday morning, they watched through the dirty window in the front hall as the older kids went off to town for their monthly visit

Alex sighed wistfully. "Ours was last week, so we have to wait another three weeks."

"Do we get any money when we go?" Penny asked, watching the bus disappear along the road.

"Twenty-five dollars," Alex said. "For those kids whose parents had an estate or some money, they get it out of that. For the rest of us, it's what the state pays the orphanage. Although we're lucky to even get twenty-five dollars once a month. I think Livè wants it all for himself. He got into big trouble a few years back when people complained about him not handing the money over."

"Who complained?" Penny asked as they walked towards the library.

"Dunno," Alex said, trailing her fingers over the wooden walls. "Some ex-staff member, or some of the kids who'd left, but didn't get any money. It was someone, because government people came here and checked the books. Livè got into big trouble, but got out of it by paying all of the money to the kids or teachers or whoever." She stopped. "Funny, it wasn't long after that that the kids started getting sick and disappearing."

They looked at each other.

"I'd never thought about that before," Alex continued, her eyes lighting up. "Paying back the money he owed must have made him poor or something. He definitely didn't like the government poking around. He made a big fuss over it and argued a lot with everyone. Like he had something to hide."

"Yeah," Penny interjected. "Everyone's money."

"He must have been keeping it for himself," Alex went on. "And then once it was all over and the money was paid back, he would have needed another income, so that's probably when the drug trials started." They reached the library and found the boys there, so Alex told them her theory.

"It makes sense," Adrian said, closing his book. "Kids did go missing not long after that raid. He drives a Ferrari, and I bet his suits are expensive because they sure look it."

"And now Mikey G is still not back, so that's eleven now," Alfred piped up.

Adrian thought about it. "I'd say it was six months. Like he had to pay it all out, and then took months to come up with another way of making money."

"So what do we do?" Alex asked. "Do we report it to someone? All the teachers might be in on it. Do we report it to the government?"

"Report what, though?" Adrian asked. "We don't even know what's happening. Whether they're only trials, or something more sinister. And who would we report it to?"

Alex sighed. "I dunno. It was just a thought."

"And it's a good one," Adrian said. "But unless we have proof of what's going on, and figure out who to tell, then there's not a whole lot we can do."

Alistair and Alfred looked up from the chessboard they'd brought in from the rec room. "You could look in the phone book."

"What for?" Penny asked.

"Governmental agencies dealing with orphanages or finances," Alfred answered.

"Or your local minister might be able to help," Alistair added.

"Unless they're in on it too," Adrian huffed. "Who knows how many people are in on this and corrupt."

"Probably only Livè," Alex said. "Especially if he doesn't want anyone else knowing after the whole fiasco of him paying back the money."

"Mmm, true," Adrian replied. "Let's see if Mikey G comes back first."

CHAPTER FOUR

Mikey G didn't come back for another week, and when he did, he looked zombified like the rest of them. Sallow complexion, sunken cheeks, hollow eyes. He barely spoke, and barely registered what was going on around him, or who was talking to him.

"We asked him a tonne of questions last night," Adrian told the group. "Where did you go, what did you do, did Livè do this to you, and all he did was mumble that he was fine and there was nothing wrong with him. He couldn't describe where he'd been, and just kept saying he was better than before."

"Clearly not," Alistair said from his seat in the library. "He's zombified like the rest of them. All gone cuckoo with whatever Livè's doing to them."

"But he didn't tell you what was happening, so we still don't know," Alex said, pulling bits of fluff from her uniform.

"We may have to find out for ourselves," Adrian mused.

"How?"

"By sneaking into his office or the basement."

They all looked at each other in shock.

"You can't be serious?" Penny asked. "We'd be caught and punished and I only just got here. I don't want to be kicked out and dumped somewhere else," she said fearfully. "I have nowhere to go."

Alex patted her hand. "We're not going to get into trouble. Are we Adrian?" She looked pointedly at him.

He shrugged. "If we want to find out what's going on so we can report him, then we might have to."

"You're the oldest, so you can do it," Penny quivered. "I have another five years here, you don't."

"I have a year left," Adrian replied. "I have a lot to lose too."

"They why don't we just leave it alone?" Penny clasped her hands.

"Because kids are being used as guinea pigs and are being left affected by whatever's happening. If they don't get treatment, proper treatment, they might end up as vegetables for the rest of their lives," Adrian said.

The girls looked at each other while the twins glanced around the room. No one wanted to say anything. No one wanted whatever was happening to go on. Someone needed to find out and put a stop to it, but who was going to do that was another matter. Each didn't want it to be them. Each wanted it to not happen to them, but the only way to stop every kid being used in drug trials was to find out what was going on, get proof, and then report it to the right authorities. But each was wondering why it was up to them to do so. Couldn't someone else do it?

*****

Later that night, when the lights were out and everyone was in bed, Alex woke Penny up. "Come on," she whispered in her ear. "Let's go search the office while everyone's asleep."

"Whuh, why?" Penny rubbed her eyes.

"Shh," Alex whispered furiously. "Don't wake anyone else up." She grabbed Penny's dressing gown.

Penny got out of bed and took her gown from Alex. They tiptoed out of the room, and after looking both ways, moved down the hallway to the stairs. They stopped, for across the open void they saw Adrian and the twins coming from the other side of the building.

Quietly, they all descended to the first floor and looked for teachers before moving down to the ground floor.

With cold concrete blocks for a floor, they tried not to scuff their slippers and make a sound. Hurriedly, they travelled down the hallway to the office and tried the handle.

"Keep a look out for the super; Livè's not here tonight. I saw him leave earlier on one of his weekends away." Adrian pulled small tools from his dressing gown pocket then slipped them into the door lock. With the others keeping an eye out, he managed to open the door and they all piled in.

"Shhh," he shushed them and closed and locked

the door behind them. "We need his office." They moved toward Livè's door and tried the handle. Locked. Adrian went to work again and managed to open it. In they stepped, and with a flick of a torch, they could see what they were doing.

"What are we looking for?" Alex whispered. "And where do we look?"

"In secret doors and cupboards. He's not about to have the info lying around with everything else," Adrian whispered back and started looking for hidden latches and cubby holes under the desk. The teens moved books, opened drawers, and looked inside containers all to no avail.

There was a jangle of keys at the main door and they all froze for a few seconds.

"Quick, lights off," Adrian whispered, flicking his torch off and pulling off his slippers. "Under the desk in the main office."

They whipped off their slippers and made it under the secretary's long large desk just as the door opened and the light flicked on.

Adrian grabbed the gas lift chair to stop it from moving and they all huddled under the desk, holding their slippers *and* their breath.

The jangle of keys moved to Livè's office and opened the door.

Adrian poked his head up and saw the super go into Livè's office and close the door. He waved Alfred and Alistair toward the open door, and they all bolted silently out the door, down the hall, and up the stairs to their floor before stopping for breath.

"We'll talk in the morning," Adrian whispered, and they all took off for their rooms as the jangle of keys came up the first set of stairs.

CHAPTER FIVE

On Sunday morning after breakfast, they donned their coats and made their way to the oval. As they did their walk around in the name of exercise, they were talking about the case and getting a good look at the surroundings, especially at the sports shed where the blood drops had led.

"So we didn't find anything last night," Adrian huffed as he walked. "Either Livè doesn't keep any evidence in his office, or we didn't have enough time to search."

"What if he keeps it down in the basement, or his room?" Alfred asked, pulling the zip of his coat down for some air.

"His room's on the top floor, so we couldn't get past the other teachers, and if it's illegal stuff then he probably keeps no record, or they are where the experiments are happening."

"And that might be the basement," Alistair said.

"Yeah, but what if it's not and it's just a basement after all?" Penny asked as they rounded the end near the shed.

"That could be true," Adrian replied. "And maybe it's all happening somewhere else entirely, but," he waved a finger, "if the trials are illegal, then why would he risk taking the kids somewhere else? At least if they are still on the premises he is telling the truth. If they are off the grounds, someone could easily find out. I think everything's happening here and it's somewhere in the basement. But what I want to know is, why did Grosvenor come to the office last night. I didn't see any alarm flashing. If there's nothing to hide in the office, why have an alarm?"

"Maybe we didn't trip an alarm; maybe Grosvenor was there for another reason," Alex said. "He did go into the office and close the door. Maybe he was up to something in there, otherwise, why close the door? If we tripped an alarm, he would have just turned on the light and looked then shut the door and left."

"Mmm," Adrian murmured. "You could be right. What did Grosvenor want in Livè's office?"

They did another lap of the oval and then moved on to the area near the sports shed.

"And all of that land belongs to the orphanage," Alex told Penny. "And there are farms over there, and town is over there, and there used to be cattle on these fields." She pointed as they made their way behind the building. "And this is the sports shed. We don't do a lot of sport in winter and the pool is closed, but it's nice for summer." Alex's voice was a little louder, and her arm movements a little wider and bigger than normal. They kept a lookout, along with the twins, while Adrian picked the lock on the back door.

"It's nice to sit out here on a cool day, especially in this spot," Alex went on. "The wind doesn't seem to come past, so it's all out of the wind and you can sit out of the cold." They glanced around.

"Got it." Adrian opened the door and they all rushed in.

Piles of sporting equipment like paddles, bats, tennis rackets, balls, nets all adorned the walls, or stuck out of large metal barrels.

"I see blood." Alistair went over to the main door and knelt down. "Drops, like in the snow last week. Dried. Not cleared up."

They looked around for more drops and found a mess of dark red brown splattered and dried.

"That's definitely not from a small wound," Alex whispered. "They wiped it up then covered it over, but it still stained the concrete."

"We don't know that it's blood," Alfred said. "Or that it's human blood."

"Let's look around some more." Adrian moved things aside on the floor to look underneath before putting it all back. The rest followed suit.

The building was long and had a door leading to the pool. They peered through the glass window in the door and noticed how decrepit the empty pool looked.

"Spooky," Penny whispered. "Like something out of a bad movie where something bad is going to happen."

A face popped up at the window.

"Aaarrgggghhh." The teens screamed and jumped back, racing for the door.

"What are you lot doing in here?" Grosvenor bellowed. They stopped at the door, facing the hulking figure that now strode toward them.

"Well?" he demanded. "You aren't allowed to be in here." His nostrils flared and his long wispy white hair now stuck up all over the place making him look like a mad scientist. "Well?"

"J-just showing Penny the sporting equipment and what we'll be doing, and the pool we'll be swimming in. She's new, you know," Alex muttered as she and Penny clung to each other.

Grosvenor eyed them all one by one. "But how did you get in? The door was locked."

Adrian gulped. "No, it wasn't."

Grosvenor leaned in close to Adrian, almost nose to nose. "I *know* it was locked. *I* locked it."

Adrian's mouth slowly opened. "But it wasn't locked," he repeated slowly.

Grosvenor eyed him some more. "Mmm, maybe the lock didn't catch. But that doesn't mean you kids can come barging in here whenever you feel like it. It might be on school grounds, but only the teachers and me are allowed." He pointedly looked at Alex and Penny. "Regardless of you wanting to show the new kid around. Now get out." He yanked open the door and pointed outside. "Get out!"

The teens pelted out of there as if the devil was after them and made a dash for the other end of the oval.

"Phew," Alex said, bending over, hands on knees, trying to catch her breath. "I was sure we were goners."

"I thought he was going to do something to us," Penny gasped, plopping down on the ground.

The boys sat down and Alistair spoke up. "I wonder if he'll dob us in to Livè?"

"Probably," Alfred replied. "He's Livè's right-hand man remember. He does everything he's told and reports back on everything else."

"But…does he?" Adrian questioned. The others looked at him. "Did he report the office incident last night? Does he actually report kids where they're not supposed to be?"

"I bet he does," Alistair said. "That's probably how they pick their next victim, because we've done something wrong."

"What did Stacey do wrong?" Penny asked. "Or Mikey G?"

"Stacey had gone to bed late and then sneaked out to the toilets, and she brought back a magazine from her shopping trip which we're not allowed to do." Alex thought back.

"And Mikey G was caught piling up on food from the dining hall to eat later that night," Alfred added.

"What about all the others?" Penny asked. "What did they do?"

Alex, Adrian and the twins thought back. It turned out, all of the kids had done something against the rules of Kingsmere.

"So they're being picked on disobeying the rules?" Penny asked. "Isn't that what we've just done?"

They all looked at each other and worried about what Penny had just said.

*****

They weren't sure whether to be truly worried or not, because for the next few weeks they kept to themselves out of Grosvenor's and Livè's way. All the same, whenever Livè was around he'd give them the evil eye. It was as if he knew what they'd been up to and was keeping an eye on them.

Penny worried more than the others because she'd been there only for four weeks and didn't want to be kicked out. Regardless of what Livè was doing, at least Penny had a roof over her head, food in her stomach, and a place to sleep.

She still missed her parents terribly and cried each night. She didn't know how she was going to get through the next five years, but if Livè got her, she would be gone. So she stuck to her work and made friends with the other girls, introducing herself and hanging out with them as well as with Alex, kept her head down, and did as she was told.

CHAPTER SIX

Their shopping day arrived and the girls and boys from each room of thirteen, fourteen and fifteen year olds all lined up in the hallway off the main door.

"Here is your money." The maths teacher handed each a crisp twenty dollar and a crisp five dollar note. "Don't lose it, don't spend it all if you don't need to, and bring back only the necessities. No magazines, no junk food, no clothes. Do you have your purses and shopping bags?"

"Yes."

"Right, now, let's go shopping."

They walked out in two rows and boarded the buses. Jumping into seats beside each other, Penny and Alex excitedly gabbled with their roommates.

"What do we do about music if we can't buy it?" Penny asked, staring out the window to see Livè staring back through the hallway window.

"Go into the music store and have a look then ask for a listen. The stores in town are used to us coming in every week, but it annoys them that we don't buy anything. We have told them we're not allowed to," Rachael said. "They don't like that either."

"And what about lunch? What do we get to eat?" Penny looked around.

"Every month we eat in a different place, but we get a lot of it at Kingsmere, burgers, chips, chicken, pizza, so we prefer stuff we don't get like cream buns and lollies," Sasha explained.

"Anything we don't get here we gorge on," Melanie said. "We do end up sick that night, or the next day sometimes, but it's worth it for once a month."

"Okay," the maths teacher yelled. "We're all on board so off we go."

Everyone cheered and they got on their way. It took them fifteen minutes to get into the bustling town of Kings Meadow.

Penny had only seen it on her way through when Mrs Grey had brought her to Kingsmere. Now she got to have a good look as they drove through and parked in a huge parking lot at the end of the main road.

"It's nine o'clock." The maths teacher, Mrs Bosely, looked at her watch. "We will be back here at four-thirty to be home by five. You will stick to each other like glue, and to your teachers like Super Glue. You will not wander off; you will not buy more than you can carry. If there is somewhere specific you want to go, tell us. If there is something specific you need, tell us. Girls, we will do your monthly shop in the supermarket after lunch."

Some of the girls giggled. "Let's get out and line up," the teacher continued.

The girls piled out of the bus and lined up two by two beside it.

"And we're off," Mrs Bosely said, leading the girls down one side of the street, while the science and chemistry teachers led the boys down the other.

Alex and the girls showed Penny everything they came across. They oohed and aahed over the dresses in store windows, listened to the latest hit single in the music store, and flicked through the latest teen magazines in the newsagent, then they all met up for lunch at the end of the street, where they indulged in cream buns and soft drink, gooey sundaes and lollies before heading off down the other side of the road.

The girls stopped in the supermarket for their necessities, stocking up when they saw it was on sale, and then all got back on the bus at four-thirty.

Mrs Bosely counted them off as they boarded, and the girls all chatted about their purchases and the pretty things they'd seen.

"It's just a pity we're not allowed to buy them," Penny said wistfully. "That blue dress was so pretty."

"It's because there's no room to store it, but if you come with no clothes then you're allowed to buy some. For those of us that bring packed bags like you," Sasha pointed at Penny, "you're not allowed to have any because you have enough."

Penny smiled softly. "My mum picked it all out for me for my birthday."

"You're lucky," Melanie said from behind them. "Your mum had great taste."

Penny's smile broadened. "Yeah, she did. She used to be a model and went into styling when she retired. She knew how to dress people in the best styles and colours."

"Except you're still growing and you'll need new clothes in a year or two when you grow out of them," Alex said.

Penny was horrified. "They're all I have. I don't want to grow out of them."

Alex shrugged. "It's gonna happen."

They arrived back just before five and ran up to their rooms to put their shopping away.

"Ugh, I feel sick," Sasha said. "Must have been the cream cakes."

"Or was it the entire bag of jelly snakes you ate during the afternoon?" Melanie asked, getting her sleepwear ready for later.

Sasha rubbed her stomach. "Might be all of it."

"So you won't want dinner?" Rachael asked.

"Ugh." Sasha flopped back on her bed. "Who can think about dinner?"

"Just rest until dinnertime and then you might feel better," Alex said. "We'll leave you alone." The girls wandered off downstairs, chatting about the day.

"So, what did you think of your first shopping day?" Alex asked Penny.

"Good," she said. "A pity it's only once a month, but I guess at least you get to see different things every time instead of getting bored with the same stuff week after week."

"I find it makes you look forward to it more," Melanie said from beside Penny. "But after a year or so it becomes the norm."

"What happens on holidays like Easter and Christmas?" Penny asked as they came to the ground floor.

"They buy us one Easter egg each and then let us have two tiny ones with dinner at night as well as a hot cross bun," Alex said.

"For Christmas we get to have tinsel and small trees in the bedroom and get turkey for lunch," Rachael added from behind them.

The girls wandered into the rec room to watch the boys playing table tennis for a few minutes before the dinner bell rang.

"I wonder if Sasha will make it down?" Melanie said before the girls parted ways.

"How was your day?" Alex asked the boys who'd been out for the day too.

"Good. Got to play the new Techra Monster Jam game at the game centre," Alfred boasted. "I won and beat everyone else, of course."

"That's because you spent nearly all your money doing so," Alistair retorted, digging into his mashed potato.

"It's not like I needed anything else," he replied. "We're not allowed to buy useful stuff, so it goes on games and junk food."

Penny watched Sasha slowly walk through the

door and over to her table. "She doesn't look good. I wonder if she'll be on Livè's radar."

The others looked too.

"Possibly," Adrian said. "Has Sasha done anything wrong?" he asked Alex.

She shrugged. "Not that I know of. Just pigged out today and now feels sick."

"Mmm," he mumbled. "That might be enough to pick her as the next victim. Better watch her the next few days."

Penny and Alex went over to the girls after dinner. "How are you, Sash?" Alex asked.

Sasha groaned. "A bit better. Mrs Slocomb gave me something to settle my stomach. That's the nurse," she added for Penny's benefit.

"How about we just all go up and rest, and chat about today some more," Penny suggested, knowing they had to keep an eye on her.

"Yeah," Sasha said. "That sounds good. I might get ready for bed early."

The girls went up and all got ready for bed, sitting and chatting some more about the day, which boys they liked, how their grades were, and what they wanted to do when they left Kingsmere.

By the time their bell rang for their bedtime they were already falling asleep.

CHAPTER SEVEN

"It's been a month since Mikey G was taken." Adrian sat down at their table the next day at lunchtime.

"And Sasha was left alone," Alex added. "So I wonder who he'll pick next."

They discussed how Livè had been around more.

"Has he been eyeing you guys?" Alex asked the twins and Adrian.

"I've seen him looking at me a few times," Adrian said.

"That's creepy," Penny said. "I've seen him standing at the end of the hallway upstairs. Like when we come down in the morning, and then he'll be there to see us all go up at night."

"I've noticed that." Adrian nodded. "And I've seen him in the hallway during class, watching through the door."

"He just stands there with his hands behind his back staring at you," Alistair butted in.

"Like now." Penny was looking at the doorway.

There stood Livè in the hall, hands clasped behind his back, his eagle eyes staring intently at the five of them.

Penny shuddered. "That's creepy," she said again and looked away.

"He's definitely staring at us all right," Alfred added. "It's definitely us."

"Yep." Adrian went back to his food. "Stop staring back and concentrate on your food."

All five kept their eyes down while they finished off their meal, and by the time it was over, Livè had gone.

*****

"Where are the twins?" Alex asked the next day when they sat down to lunch and she noticed Al and Al missing.

"Sickroom," Adrian said. "Didn't feel good after breakfast, so went to get something from the nurse."

"Maybe we should go and visit them after we eat," Penny said. "Make sure they really are sick."

"And still in the sick room," Alex added.

They got permission from the teacher to go and visit the twins, but only had a few minutes before class.

"How are Alistair and Alfred doing?" Adrian asked when they got there.

Mrs Slocomb looked up in surprise. "They're doing better, so I sent them up to bed just a few seconds before you arrived."

Adrian glanced at Penny and Alex. "We didn't see them. Must have missed them. Thanks."

They backed out of the room and closed the door.

"That's strange," Adrian whispered. "Come on." They rushed for the stairs and took them two at a time, but Penny and Alex skidded to a halt at the boys' side of the building because they weren't allowed to be in the boys' wing. Adrian bolted down to their room and flew inside. A few seconds later he emerged and shook his head.

Penny and Alex looked at each other; both fearful Livè had got to them.

Adrian flew from room to room and checked the bathroom, shaking his head, he rushed back to the girls. "They're not there."

"In any of the rooms?" Alex asked.

"In none of them," Adrian said. "Nowhere. We didn't pass them, didn't run into them. They're not anywhere."

The three teens stood staring at each other as the bell rang.

"Maybe they'll turn up in class," Alex said as they made their way back down for their lesson. "Let us know later if they turn up."

*****

Penny's stomach started gurgling during history class, and she wrapped her arms around herself to mask the sound. Taking slow deep breaths, she tried to calm it. The girl in front of her turned around to look, and Penny faintly smiled back.

Penny glanced over at Alex to find her face

screwed up in agony.

"Miss," the girl in front of Penny called out. "I think these two are going to be sick."

Alex laid her head on the table. "Ugh," she groaned.

"Why don't you girls go to the sickroom? Mrs Slocomb can give you something."

The girls glanced at each other, fearful after Alistair and Alfred's disappearance.

"I don't want you being sick in my classroom," the teacher said. "So go." She pointed to the doorway and Penny and Alex reluctantly rose from behind their desks.

Clutching one another's hands, they slowly made their way out of the room, down the hall, and into the sickroom.

"Oh dear, two more sick. Looks like the start of an outbreak." Mrs Slocomb hustled them over to two single beds. "I'll take your temperature and check your pulse." She got to work, and after checking their breathing and temperatures, gave them injections. "It's for the nausea."

"Ow!" Alex jumped at the jab and rubbed her arm.

"Hush now," Mrs Slocomb said as she advanced on Penny. "You'll start feeling better soon. Just lie down and let it work."

The girls lay down while the injection took effect and soon found themselves drifting off.

CHAPTER EIGHT

Adrian barged into the dining hall at dinnertime to find his usual table empty. This was not unusual, as sometimes the girls turned up late. But with the twins gone, he wasn't sure. Getting his food, he thought the girls would be there, but he found himself eating alone.

This isn't good, he thought and quickly finished off his meal before going over to the girls' classmates. "Do you girls know where Alex and Penny are?"

The girls stared wide-eyed as the five foot ten, blue eyed brunet all the girls dreamt about stood beside their table.

Finally, Sasha spoke up. "They weren't feeling well in class, so they were sent to the sick room."

That piqued Adrian's curiosity. "Thanks," he muttered and asked one of the teachers for permission to go and visit.

A few minutes later he was standing in the sick room where the only person was Mrs Slocomb. "I came to see how Alex and Penny are. Did they have the same problem as the twins?"

"Upset stomachs," Mrs Slocomb said, bustling around. "Gave them a nausea injection and they slept for a bit. Sent them up to their room just before you got here."

"Thanks." Adrian hustled out of the room and quickly made his way up the stairs to the girls' wing. He stopped. Boys weren't allowed to be up there, and if he was caught, God knows what would happen to him. Nevertheless, he needed to find Alex and Penny.

After peering over the balustrade to see if any teachers were around, he raced from room to room checking as he didn't know which room they slept in. Not that it mattered. There was no one on the floor, and he made it back downstairs as the bell rang.

He had to find them.

Going through room after room he looked, he asked, and he checked, finally ending up in the basement. None of them was in the laundry room, and besides the super's and storage room, there was only one room left.

He saw the shadow of Grosvenor behind the glass and decided to leave the room until after bedtime. He ran upstairs, grabbed his torch and coat, and managed to make his way down to the sports shed by the light of the moon.

Going round back so no one saw his light; he picked the lock and found his way in. He flicked on his torch and searched, but it was obvious they weren't there. On arriving at the door that led to the pool, he picked that lock and made his way in. The room was cavernous in the semi-darkness with a great hulking empty pit in the middle.

He swung his torch back and forth as he walked, softly calling out their names so as not to draw attention. "Alistair, Alfred…Penny…Alex…"

He checked in all the cupboards, and quickly glanced over the pool, but the only things there were some filthy black water, a couple of broken chairs, trash, and a few rats.

Without giving it a thorough check over, he left through the same door he'd entered after completing a circuit of the pool, completely missing the decomposing corpse with its wide eyes, bare teeth, and dismembered body dumped in the black filth that was the water at the bottom of the deep end.

The wide eyes stared up at the ceiling as maggots and insects feasted on the young ten year old flesh that lay rotting under the water.

*****

Adrian made it out of the shed and decided to do a quick search of the grounds. Moving by the moonlight, he kept his torch usage to a minimum. He briskly walked up and around the front looking for basement windows or something that would provide a clue. He crunched across the front drive and around the other side of the forbidding building, pulling his coat around him to keep out the freezing winter cold. He found his way back to the back door and was able to make it in without being detected.

Quickly checking in every room, he headed for his own room to see if the twins were back, stopping to ask Penny and Alex's roommates if they'd seen the girls since dinner.

It was nos all round and Adrian left his coat on his bed. There was only one place left to look besides all of the teachers' rooms and Livè's office, but there was no way he'd hide kids in there. So there really was only one place left to go, and that was the room at the end of the basement hall.

*****

Adrian waited until all of the kids were in bed, and all of the lights had been turned off, then waited some more. He waited until his bedside clock struck midnight before he climbed out of bed as quietly as he could. He'd remained fully clothed, so he could have a quick getaway and didn't waste time dressing. He sneaked out into the hallway and down the stone steps to the ground floor, pausing occasionally to listen for a teacher, or Grosvenor, just in case he was lurking.

Having made his way toward the basement door, Adrian paused before turning the knob. Slowly, he opened the door and closed it behind him, then quietly descended the stairs. All was silent in the laundry room, super's room, and storage room. But the room at the end of the hallway was not.

The hall was dimly lit. Adrian wished he'd brought his torch, but he couldn't be noticed and didn't need the attention. He crept up to the boiler room door, grasped the handle, and turned it.

Expecting the door to be locked, he was surprised when it wasn't, and it opened noiselessly. He peered through the two inch gap, but didn't see Grosvenor. He pushed the door open, sneaked in, and silently closed it behind him before hiding behind the big machinery to his left. He searched the room for any sign of the others, but saw only pipes and machines; everything that kept the orphanage running.

He silently moved along the wall behind the machinery until he came to another door at the back of the room. It was hidden by a large mass of pipe work, and no one would know it existed unless they looked. He put his ear to the door before trying the handle which turned easily.

"Ah!" His hand slapped his neck expecting a mosquito, but all he saw when he turned his head was Dr Livè holding a syringe with Grosvenor grinning right behind him.

"And that makes a little quintet," Livè said. "That will stop the nausea in no time. Such a pity you're sick."

Adrian's eyes closed and he slumped to the floor.

CHAPTER NINE

Penny came to.

Her eyes blinked slowly under the bright white light and she pushed herself up onto her elbow. "Where am I?"

She swung her legs over the side of the camp bed she was lying on and planted her feet on the floor. "Hello?"

She felt groggy, slow, as if her head was full of cotton wool. She couldn't think straight. "Hello… Alex?"

Standing, she waited until the sudden dizziness left her. "Alex?"

The lone white globe above her was alone no more. Light after light flicked on all around the room to show her reflection in at least fifty mirrors.

Fifty Pennys looked back.

"What? What's going on?" She panicked. "Alex?" she yelled, running for the nearest mirror and pounding on it. "Alex?"

Mirror after mirror she banged on, running around the room in circles looking for a door handle so she might get out of this crazy carnival sideshow.

"Alex," she screamed and fifty Pennys screamed it right back at her. "Help, someone help me. I'm in here."

Round and around she ran, banging, screaming, yelling for help, all to no avail. She collapsed onto the camp bed and curled into a little ball, sobbing for all the months of pain, all the months of heartache, all the months of loneliness; only to end up in some crazy room of mirrors alone, lonely, without her parents, Alex, Adrian or the twins to help her. No one. No one to help her. She was all alone. With no one to help her.

Penny knew her days were at an end. That *she* was at an end. There was no way she was going to get out, or survive, and so she cried harder.

Her psychological breakdown began.

*****

Alex woke up on her own camp bed in the middle of her own room with one light bulb in the centre.

She stood unsteadily, and was then blinded by the fifty or so light bulbs that lit up the room. "What the hell!"

She looked before her, all around her, each wall had a staircase, multiple staircases, going up, going down, they zigzagged up and down walls.

"If that's the way it's gonna be then," she said and barrelled up the first set of stairs without a thought.

Banging on walls looking for a way out, Alex went up every stair and down every stair. She kicked, she banged, she stopped until exhaustion overtook her and she collapsed onto the camp bed.

"*What is going on here?*" she asked out loud, half expecting a voice to come booming into the room. "Livè, is that you? Is this what you've done to all of the other kids you've experimented on? Is this where you hide them until you send them back? *Answer me, damn it!*"

Receiving no answer, she went to work again, this time studying and running her fingers over the cracks and crevices in the stairs, tapping, knocking, trying to figure out if the walls were solid or had nothing behind them. If they had nothing…maybe she could break them…

*****

Alistair stared up at the ceiling. He'd spent a few hours trying to get out of his tomb and was now resting on his camp bed in the middle of the room. He'd already figured out that the doorways that kept appearing led straight back into the room. It seemed to be built in a circle. When one door opened he dived for it, running through the tunnel as though his life depended on it, and when he thought he'd found another door and went through it, he was right back in his room. It was a cell that was going to keep him running around in circles for as long as he was there.

"Just like a rat," he muttered, trying to come up with a way of getting out. *I wonder where Al is and if anyone is looking for us?*

*****

Alfred was snoring his head off. While he'd spent a few hours trying to get out of his tomb, a room whose walls kept closing in on him and going in and out, he'd decided to not bother with any of it and just sleep.

CHAPTER TEN

Adrian finally woke.

He came to under a bright light and tried to rub his eyes, but couldn't move his hands. "Mmm." He glanced down at them to find wide leather straps bound them to the chair arms.

He lifted his head, but found it restrained. His feet were bound to the bottom. *It's a dentist's chair*, he thought. *Why would I be strapped to a dentist's chair?* He blinked a few times to clear his vision and saw Livè come up to him.

"Ah, you're awake." He waved a big long syringe near Adrian's face. "Time for some fun."

Lights flicked on around the room and walls suddenly became clear.

Adrian could see Alex in a room to his left and Alistair in a room to his right. Both of them were spinning around looking at the walls that had suddenly evaporated.

"Wake up children," Livè called. "Time to see what's really been happening here at Kingsmere Orphanage."

The sound of the doctor's voice had roused Alfred from his sleep and Penny from her comatose state. All of them plastered themselves against the glass to see Livè standing over Adrian who was strapped into a chair.

The five rooms were in a pentagon shape around a central room that contained machinery full of wires and switches.

Livè had Adrian in another room ready to do whatever it was he got up to.

Alistair and Alfred stood staring, unmoving, unsure of what to do, for they had never encountered such horror before. Shocked expressions plastered themselves on their faces.

Alex pounded on the glass yelling for Livè to stop, to let them out, to let them go. She wasn't going down without a fight and she was ready for it.

Penny stood dumbstruck, fearful as silent tears flowed down her poor little cheeks at how her life was about to end. With a terrified, pathetic whimper, she scampered back to her bed, curled up in a ball, clamped her eyes shut, and wrapped her arms around her head to block out the horrors that had befallen her. "I'm coming Mummy and Daddy," she barely whispered. "I'll see you soon."

Adrian squirmed in the chair. "You won't get away with this Livè. We'll tell everyone what you've done. That you let drug companies trial their drugs on us, and that you're taking big fat payouts for it."

Livè's laugh echoed through the chamber. "Drug trials," he bellowed. "Is that what you think this is?"

Adrian's eyes moved to the syringe in his hand. "Isn't that what you're holding? Drugs?"

Livè glanced amusedly at the syringe and then at Adrian. "It's not drugs, my dear boy, and I'm not doing drug trials." He leaned menacingly over Adrian. "What I'm doing, boys and girls, are trials of another nature. Experiments if you will. Experiments of a very different nature to drug trials. Why do you think children come back in a worse state than before?" He laughed again, manically this time. "Because I do experiments on them with all kinds of implements." His laugh echoed around the sub-basement as he lowered the needle to Adrian's eye.

HANTEL AND GRESEL: FOOD CRITICS

CHAPTER ONE

"Hantel, why don't you und Gresel go und play in de woods today," Mrs Grudebaker suggested to her son. She wiped her hands nervously on the ratty old hand towel in the ratty old kitchen. "I don't have any food to give you, but you could pick some fruit from de trees und berries from de bushes."

"But, Mama," Hantel replied, picking at the holes in his lederhosen. "We've been told not to go into de woods." He sat on the floor playing with the straw man doll he had made.

"Und who told you dat?" She pulled out a kitchen chair that her husband had found by the side of the road. Their household furniture was sparse as they had no money to afford new or even nice things, so everything came from other people dumping it by the roadside.

"De mayor announced it last week in de city square." He watched his mother. "You were dere Mama, you heard him too."

"Well." She fussed with her ratty old apron. "Dings have changed und it's now okay for kinder to go into de woods again."

Hantel wondered what his mother was up to, and why she was so eager for him and his sister to go into the woods.

"Why don't you take dis basket und bring some fruit for us." She gathered the basket and a couple of ratty towels. "Wrap up de fruit so it stays nice, und bring it home for us."

Hantel's stomach growled. *You're just being silly,* he told himself. *Mama only wants us to collect some fruit so we can eat und have supper. Nodding else.* "Okay, Mama, I will go und find Gresel."

"Dat's a gut boy." She patted him on the head as he hugged her. "Gutbye, my son, take care of your sister." After handing him the basket, she watched him call to his sister who joined him in the front yard. They both waved goodbye and skipped hand in hand along the road that led to the woods.

She fretted. "Oh, dear, how could I have done dis? I can't, I cannot do dis."

Mr Grudebaker came out from the bedroom and heard his wife's comment. Patting her on the shoulder he consoled her. "Dere, dere, it had to be done. We have nein money, nein food, und now we lose dis house. We had to let de kinder go."

Mrs Grudebaker sobbed and wiped the tears streaming down her face. "It doesn't mean I have to like it or agree wid it."

*****

Completely unaware of what was really going on, and why Mama had sent them into the woods, Hantel and Gresel skipped gaily down the dirt road, holding hands, and swinging the basket as they went.

"Hullo, Mrs Gunderson," Gresel called, stopping to chat with their neighbour.

"Hullo, Gresel," Mrs Gunderson replied. "How are you zwei today?" She was sweeping her front porch and pathway to her pretty white mailbox, sitting on her pretty white picket fence.

"Gut, danke, Mrs Gunderson," Hantel said, standing beside his sister. He and Gresel were twins and didn't go anywhere without one another.

"Und where are you zwei off to today?" she asked, resting on her broom.

"We're off to de woods to collect some fruit. We're hungry, und Mama und Papa have nein food." Hantel showed her the basket. "We're bringing it back for supper."

A worried frown slid down Mrs Gunderson's face. "Into de forest?" she said. "Why would your Mama send you into de forest, when just last week we were being told to keep our kinder out of de forest?"

Hantel frowned in return. "I reminded Mama of dat, but she said dere wasn't anyding to worry about. Dat it was all over."

Mrs Gunderson studied the children before her. Anorectic-thin, they had sallow complexions, haunted eyes. They were dressed in secondhand hand-me-downs their mother had managed to acquire even though they were almost worn through. She understood the burden and knew how hard it must have been for Mrs Grudebaker to do.

"Of course, kinder, I had forgotten about dat. Of course it's safe. I hope you get lots of fruit for your supper. Gutbye now." She waved and scuttled back inside her own pretty house with her own pretty things, and peered through her own pretty curtains to watch the puzzled expressions on the children's faces before they skipped off down the road.

"Dat was weird," Gresel said, skipping alongside her brother. "Why was Mrs Gunderson so forgetful?"

"Don't know." Hantel stopped skipping for they had come to the edge of the woods and they stood staring up at the huge green trees.

"I'm scared, Hantel." Gresel shivered and inched closer to her brother. Looking through the forest, she could barely see any more than twenty or so feet. The shrubbery was so thick not much light was streaming in.

"Dere's nein need to be scared, Gresel." Hantel tightened his grip on his sister. "I'm here. I will protect you. Come, we must go."

This time there was no skipping, just silent walking, hand in hand, left foot in front of right, right foot in front of left, until Hantel stopped to investigate a tree.

"All of de fruit has been picked," he said, scouring the ground around the tree. "Looks like odder kinder have been here." Standing, he glanced around. "Looks like we will have to go furder into de woods."

"Oh, Hantel…" Gresel's voice shook. "I don't want to. It's so dark in dere, und scary looking." She hid her face in her raggedy doll.

"Come, Gresel," Hantel said. "We must find food." Grabbing his sister's hand, he moved on with her, pretending he was older and bigger than he actually was.

They walked for what seemed like forever, which to a ten year old wouldn't be very far, until they came across trees and bushes brimming with an abundance of fruit all ripe for the picking.

"Dere, Gresel, start filling up de basket." Hantel set it down under a tree. "I'll get de apples, you get de berries. Quickly now, und don't wander far, stay near me." He quickly yanked apple after apple from the tree while Gresel picked delicious blackberries from the bushes nearby. Soon, their basket was brimming over with ripe succulent fruit.

"We must get more," Hantel said, eyeing his sister's apron. "Take dat off und fill it, den we will tie it up."

While she took off her apron, Hantel gathered more berries and laid them on the apron before expertly tying opposite corners together to form a bundle.

"Now we must go." He looked up at the sky. "It looks like it's getting dark. We must get home before de sun sets."

Holding hands, they quickly followed the path back through the forest to the road. Once there, they raced down the road until they came to their house.

Barging through the door, Hantel ran into the kitchen and placed the basket on the table. "Mama, we're home, look what we found." He piled up the berries and apples on the table. "Red juicy apples und luscious blackberries." He turned to see Mrs Grudebaker in the doorway looking ever so surprised.

Gresel looked up from her seat at the table. "Hullo, Mama, look what we got."

"But-but-but," Mrs Grudebaker stuttered. "You were supposed to be…" Her hand flew to her mouth. "Oh," she cried and enveloped her children into her embrace. "You're back." Hugging and kissing them, she didn't see her husband come home.

"What do we have here?" he yelled, stomping a foot. "You weren't meant to come back."

"Yet." Mrs Grudebaker flashed her husband a warning. "You weren't meant to come back yet. We dought you would be much longer. So, what do we have here?" She picked up a berry and popped it into her mouth and chewed. Her face puckered and she spat the berry out. "Ew, dat is awful, sour it is, sour. Why did you bring back bad food?" She bit into an apple and a worm popped out. She spat it out next to the berry. "Hantel und Gresel," she wiped her mouth, "why did you bring back rotten fruit? We cannot eat dis."

"But it's not, Mama," Hantel defended. "We ate some while we were picking und dey were sweet und juicy. Let me try." He popped several berries into his mouth and the sweet sugary goodness dripped down his throat until he swallowed. "Dey are sweet, Mama, try dese." He handed some to his mother who suspiciously put them in her mouth and chewed.

"Pleh!" Out they came. "How can you say dose are sweet, Hantel? Dey are horrible und sour. Where did you get dem from?"

Hantel and Gresel shrank back against the wall of the tiny kitchen. The glares from their Mama and Papa were scaring them as were their raised voices.

"From de woods, Mama. Where you told us to go, but dere was nein fruit dere, so we went furder until we came to dis clearing dat had all kinds of fruit."

"Well, it's rotten," she spat. "Und can't be eaten. We will just have to chuck it all out und go widout any food at all." She swept the fruit into the basket, walked outside, and dumped it all in the rubbish pile.

Hantel and Gresel watched in horror. There was nothing wrong with the food as they had tasted much of it, so for Mama to say there was something wrong with it was wrong. Had Mama gotten some rotten pieces, but they had not? Had Mama's taste buds changed? Who knew, but they watched Mama come back in and waited quietly until she spoke.

"Tomorrow you will go back into de forest und find more fruit. Go in furder, deeper. Get de gut stuff, und make sure," she said as she towered over her frightened children, "you get sweet fruit, not rotten. Now, you can go to bed widout any dinner."

Hantel and Gresel made their way out of the kitchen and into the small room they shared.

"Why would Mama drow out such gut food?" Hantel asked as he slipped on his nightgown.

Gresel rushed out the door and returned with her apron that she'd left in the hallway. Some of the berries had leaked and made her apron stained, but she laid it out on the floor and untied it. "I don't know Hantel, but we will not go to bed widout food."

They devoured half of the berries and left the other half for breakfast. Lying in bed with full stomachs, they had the best sleep they'd ever had.

CHAPTER TWO

In the morning their Mama woke them, demanding they get up and get more food. They got dressed and rushed out the door, and when they were out of sight, finished off the berries they'd hidden in the basket. They waved black stained hands at a surprised Mrs Gunderson who stood with broom in hand ready to sweep her front porch. As they came to the end of the road they stopped.

"Hantel, do you remember where we went? We don't want to get lost," Gresel said, clinging to her raggedy doll that now had blackberry stains on it.

"Of course," he replied. "We stick to de pad und follow it in und den out. Let's go."

They quickly entered the forest and travelled the same route they had taken the day before, and quickly came upon the clearing with its fruit trees and berry bushes. Tasting some berries and munching into an apple as they worked, they loaded the basket.

"Mama said to go deeper, Hantel, but I don't want to." Gresel popped a berry into her mouth and then offered one to her dolly.

"I know." Hantel pulled some apples from the

tree. "We will go a little furder und den head back. Come." He picked up the basket and took his sister's hand. "Just a little furder."

They walked along the path that led away from the clearing. Brambles and vines caught in their hair and tugged at their tatty clothes. They weren't sure how far they'd walked when they came into an open space full of berry bushes and sparkling apple trees.

"Oh, Hantel, what is all dat stuff growing on de trees?" Gresel pointed to orange balls hanging from a tree.

Hantel picked one and bit into it. "Ew." He spat out the orange rind. "Dat is horrible." He licked his fingers. "Mmm, but dat is gut." Pulling apart the orange, he tasted the juicy pulp inside. "Mmm, it's gut, Gresel, try some." He handed the other half to her and she sucked on it.

"Mmm, it's sweet." She finished it off and picked another, pulling it apart and sucking it dry. "Mmm, so gut, Hantel, so gut."

While Gresel ate the orange balls, Hantel sampled other fruit. Berries in all shades, red, pink, yellow, blue. He tried them all and added them to the basket.

After filling their basket, and themselves, with fruit, the twins headed off home to a very surprised set of parents.

"Mama, we're home, we found more fruit," Hantel called as he and Gresel slipped through the door.

Gresel ran off to hide her apron full of fruit in

their room, and Hantel took the basket to the kitchen where he found his Mama white as a ghost and sitting at the table.

"Mama, are you all right?" Hantel asked, looking into the pale face of his mother. "We brought more fruit, different kinds, here." He pulled open an orange. "Try dis." He sucked some, murmuring, "mmm sweet und juicy."

Mrs Grudebaker stumbled back from her chair and against the cupboard. "What are you…why are you…what are you doing here? You were supposed to go into de woods…furder, deeper…you were supposed to go…"

Hantel was puzzled. "We did, Mama. Dat is how we found de odder fruit trees. Dere is a clearing beyond de first."

Gresel came into the kitchen and sat down on the other chair. "What happened to de odder chairs?" she asked. "Und de cupboard in our room?"

Mrs Grudebaker snapped out of her trance. "We had to sell de cupboard for food, und burn de chairs for de fire."

Hantel was hurt. "What will we put our clodes in now? I liked dat cupboard."

"What does it matter?" his mother snapped. "You don't have many clodes anyway. Und what is dis?" She picked up the orange and tried it. "Ew, it is sour Hantel. You brought us bad food again."

"Nein, Mama, I didn't." He watched her throw it on the floor and try berries. They went the same way as the orange.

"Dose are all bad, Hantel." She swept them into the basket and dumped it all outside in the rubbish pile as she had the night before.

"Mama, dere is nodding wrong wid dis food," Hantel pleaded. "Dey are sweet. Maybe you are not giving dem a chance und your tastebuds are not healdy."

Mrs Grudebaker turned in rage. "How dare you say dere is someding wrong wid me. I know sour when I taste it. Und dat fruit you have been collecting is *not sweet*. It's sour, und you are a bad boy for lying to me und trying to trick me wid your fruit. Go to bed. Go to bed und don't come out until tomorrow when you will go back into de woods und not come out until you can find decent food to eat. How *dare you* lie to me. Go to bed, you will not get any supper."

Hantel and Gresel stood there in shock while their mother towered over them. What was wrong with Mama for her to say such things? Why was she so angry?

"*Go to bed,*" she thundered, and they took off running.

Huddled in their tiny room, in their tiny bed, under the one blanket they had, they discussed Mama's reaction until Papa came home, hoping he would come in and fix the situation. But, he didn't, and waiting until their parents had gone to sleep did they gorge on the berries that Gresel had hidden in their room when they'd come home.

CHAPTER THREE

The next morning, after not seeing Papa, and being sent off by a very stern Mama, the twins walked morosely down the road toward the forest. Mama had demanded more fruit, after wasting two delicious bounties, and they had to go further into the woods. Munching on apples saved from the night before, they made their way down the path, through the first clearing, along the second path, and into the sparkling second clearing.

Hantel picked an orange and ate it, listening to the birds tweet and the water rush by.

Water!

"Gresel, do you hear dat? It sounds like rushing water." Hantel pushed his way through thick bushes and vines to come upon a small babbling brook. He knelt down and tasted the water. It was cool, crisp and delicious. "Have some, Gresel, it is so gut."

While Gresel drank, Hantel scoured the grounds. He wasn't sure where the brook had come from, but decided to see where it led. "Come, Gresel, we shall follow de brook."

Holding hands, they followed the brook downstream until they came to a small clearing that sparkled so brightly they had to cover their eyes. In the field to their left sat a little house all brightly decorated. Smoke curled up from the chimney, and a white picket fence spread around it.

"Whoa," Hantel said. "Let's go see who lives dere."

"Nein." Gresel pulled back, fear covering her pretty face.

"Don't be scared." Hantel pulled her along. "I'm here."

They made their way up the path and through the gate, stopping in awe at the sight of the giant brown toadstools in the yard. Step by step, they approached the house, noticing the bright colours on the walls.

Hantel stopped and pointed to the front wall beside the porch. "Does dat look like food? Like sweets from de sweet shop?" He walked over and pushed one. "It's soft." He licked his finger. "It's sweet." He ran his tongue over the soft jubes on the wall. "Yum."

Gresel joined him and tasted a sweet. "It's sherbet."

"Oh, look, they come off." Hantel pulled several sweets off the wall and stuck them in his mouth. "Mmm, gut…"

They ploughed their way through half a wall before noticing the hunched over little old grey-haired lady in her black dress and white apron standing on her porch watching them.

"Um!" Gulp. Hantel jumped back and quickly swallowed the mouthful of candy.

"Enjoying my house?" she asked with a twinkle in her eye.

Gresel stared wide-eyed. "Um…" Gulp. "Ja."

"We're sorry." Hantel wiped his mouth. "Dis is your house? But it is made of candy."

"Ja," the old woman replied. "It is." She stood watching the two children with their long blond hair and big blue eyes hanging on to each other for grim death. "But dat does not mean you can eat it."

Hantel gulped again. "We are sorry. We are hungry, und Mama und Papa sent us into de woods to get fruit as we do not have any food. Dey told us to go furder dan ever before und dat is how we found de stream. We followed it und found your house. We did not know anyeins lived here in de woods." Hantel was feeling just a little bit sick after devouring so many sweets.

The old woman studied them. "Ja, ja, always kinder und always starving." She clasped her wrinkled old hands in front of her. "Parents always send deir starving youngsters into de woods for food. Many end up here."

The sun shone down on the little house in the sparkling clearing.

"Are you still hungry?" She licked her lips. "I have a huge pot of soup on de fire. You can have some if you like." She waved them in as she walked inside.

"Hantel," Gresel whispered. "I'm not too sure about dis. I'm scared."

Hantel looked at his sister. "It's all right, Gresel, I'll look after you. It's just a little old lady. What harm could she do?"

They slowly entered the little candy house in the sparkling clearing to find themselves in a large spacious kitchen diner.

"Come, make yourselves at home," the old woman said, pointing to the dining table to their left. "I'll get you a big bowl of soup." She fussed around while they took their seats, laying the table with cutlery, napkins, and a tablecloth. After heaping great big ladles of hot steaming soup into bowls, she laid them before the twins. "Eat up. Fill up dose empty tummies of yours." She sat by the fire with her knitting, watching the children.

Hantel and Gresel slowly picked up their spoons and blew on the hot soup. Tasting it, they found it not to be to their liking.

"What is in dis?" Hantel asked, laying down his spoon.

"You don't like it?" the old lady asked in surprise, dropping her knitting into her lap.

Gresel politely held her hands in her lap while letting her brother do all the talking. She hadn't liked it either, but it was not her place to say so.

"Well," Hantel started, not wanting to sound ungrateful. "It doesn't have much taste to it. It is just water und root vegetables. I cannot taste any salt. How long have you cooked it for?"

The old woman stared at him in surprise. "How do you know about dings like dat?" She looked toward the huge cauldron. So large that several children could ever so easily fit inside. It took up most of the space in the kitchen.

"I learned from Mama," Hantel replied.

"I did put salt in it," she continued, gazing intently at him.

"But did you put enough for de amount of water you are using?"

The light dawned on the old woman. "Nein, nein, I did not." She hastily got up, picked up the bag of salt, and prepared to pour it in.

"Nein, nein, stop," Hantel yelled. "You must calculate de amount." He walked over to her and took the bag. "How much water is in de pot?"

Her surprised expression continued. "At least eins tausend buckets."

Now it was Hantel's turn to be surprised. "Eins tausend buckets of water? Dat is a lot. Well den, you must calculate einhundert grams of salt for every eins tausend buckets of water. So dat is ein tausend grams of salt for eins tausend buckets. Do you have scales?"

The old woman looked around. "Ja, ja, in de corner." She pointed to the antique scales sitting on the corner bench.

Hantel went over and found a bowl. He weighed it, calculated the difference, and started pouring salt into it. He found he could only get drei hundert grams at a time into the bowl so handed it over to the woman to pour into the cauldron. "Do you remember how much you put in originally?"

"Eins big scoop," she said, handing back the bowl.

Hantel measured what one big scoop was and found it to be at least funf hundert grams. "Well, wid de funf you put in und de drei we just added, we only need zwei more." He measured, added, and gave the cauldron a mix before tasting. "Ah, dat's better. At least wid taste. Try it."

The old lady dipped the spoon in and tried the broth which was thicker now. "Ja, ja, dat is better."

Hantel took some salt over to Gresel's and his bowls, sprinkling some into each. "Dis should taste better now." They gave it a mix and tried it again.

"Mmm, dat is better," Gresel said and they devoured their soup quickly.

"Would you like dessert?" the old woman asked, pulling a pink tart from a metal box in the ground.

"Why do you keep it in de ground?" Hantel eyed off the strawberries on the pie.

"Dere is an underground spring on dat side und it keeps the metal cool enough for me to store food," she said, pulling a big knife from her pocket and sliding it through the luscious looking pie. She plated each piece and slid them towards the children. "From de berries in de forest. Tell me what you dink."

The twins picked up their forks and took their first bite. Gresel screwed her face up.

"You do not like?" the old woman fretted. She had never come across children who had not liked her food before and so this was perplexing her.

Hantel laid down his fork. "De berries are tart, sour, de crumbly base is too fatty, it's sticking to my palette."

"Mmm," the old lady mumbled. "I did not dink to add sugar to de berries as dey are sweet enough."

"Did you reduce dem in a pan on low heat, or just mash dem up und put dem into de base?" Hantel picked at his piece with his fork. "Dat would make a difference."

"Well, I just mashed dem up und put some homemade red jelly in wid it. Und made de base from flour, eggs und lard."

"Too much lard." Hantel nodded. "De berries need sugar, und whatever dat jelly was, it's not very nice."

"Mmm…" The old woman gathered the plates. "Seems like you could teach me a ding or zwei about cooking. Would you like someding else for dessert?"

"Some berries from de clearing would be fine," Hantel said, disappointed that a woman of senior years who should know how to cook by now would not know such basic things in the kitchen.

Gresel had a sheepish look on her face as she kicked Hantel under the table.

He raised a brow.

"You wanted someding else, dear?" The old woman placed a bowl of berries in front of them.

Gresel blushed. "May we…um…"

"Speak up, Kind."

"May we have some sweets for dessert?"

The old woman laughed gaily while Hantel frowned and shook his head.

"Of course you can," she said. "Go outside und try everyding you see, even de toadstools, dey are made of cake."

With wide eyes and open mouths, Hantel and Gresel raced outside and stuck their tongues on everything they came across.

The toadstools were deliciously soft chocolate cake that melted in their mouths. The white picket fence was fruit cake. The trees were soft mint leaf jubes. The rocks and pebbles were hard sugar candies, and the house itself was gingerbread with candy on top, as were the window shutters.

"Enjoy yourselves, kinder," the old woman called from the porch. She watched them run around, tasting, licking, trying everything, starting the beginning of their crack sugar addiction. *Ja,* she thought, *dey will do nicely, but how could dey know about food so? De boy said his Mama taught him, und he knew how to make my soup better. He even said my pie could have been made differently to make it sweeter. Maybe I should keep dem around for a while?*

Hantel and Gresel ate as much as they could before slumping down on the porch.

"Mmm, full…" Hantel mumbled.

"Ja," Gresel added, rubbing her stomach. "Me too."

"Why don't you kinder come inside und lie down on de bed? It will be much more comfortable," the old woman crooned.

"Nein," a sleepy Hantel said. "We should be getting home to Mama und Papa soon."

"But we have nodding to take back, Hantel," Gresel reminded him. "We cannot go back widout any food."

"Mmm," Hantel murmured, his eyes half closed.

"We must take back food."

"Why don't you come inside und have a nap, und I will have a basket full of food ready for you when you wake?" the old woman said. "Come, come…come inside for a nap." She ushered them into a small bedroom off the kitchen and they huddled on the big soft bed. "Sweet dreams, kinder, dere will be plenty of food for you when you wake."

She watched them drift off to sleep before closing the door. "Ja, sweet dreams, kinder, for when you wake you will not remember where you are from, or who your Mama und Papa are." She busied herself tidying up and stirring the soup. The meat was now falling off the bones and the eyeballs gave it the extra flavour and texture it needed.

"Ja, just needed time und more salt." She tasted it. "But how did de boy know dat? I wonder if I could keep dem to try recipes out on. De Strudelbaker Falls Bake-Off is coming, und he could help me perfect my recipe."

She looked in the mirror on the wall opposite the cauldron. "I need to get my hair done to look presentable." She patted the long matted grey mess. "Und I need to get my pretty dress washed und ironed. Mmm, I wonder which recipe I should use."

She spent the next hour mulling over her recipes until the children woke. "Ah, dere you are, how was your nap?" She watched the twins stumble out of the room. "De washroom is de little building outside if you want to wash up."

"Ja, Grandmama, we will go und do dat," they

said and wandered off outside to wash up.

She didn't need to worry about them wandering off or going back home now. The spell she had put on the soup made the children think she was their grandmother, and that they had lived there all of their lives. They came back in and gathered around her at the table.

"What are you doing, Grandmama?" Gresel asked.

"Trying to come up wid de perfect recipe for de Strudelbaker Falls Bake-Off," she said. "We must come up wid a recipe dat will knock everyeins's lederhosen off." She flipped through her cookbook. "De winner gets zehn marks. Hantel, help me pick someding out. We must perfect it by next week."

They sat talking about recipes until dinnertime when Grandmama served them soup for dinner. She made sure to keep any bits and pieces they may recognise away from them, and found Hantel in particular liked the taste.

"It's much better now, ja," he said.

"Dat's because de meat has fallen off de bone," Grandmama replied. "So now de fluid has been infused wid de essence of de meat."

The twins hungrily ate and tried an apple pie for dessert.

"Mmm." Hantel looked up at the ceiling while trying to decipher the flavours of the pie. "Not bad…de apples need a little someding, und de pastry has too much lard. You really should lay off de lard, Grandmama," he scolded her. "It's *very* fattening."

The old woman raised a brow. "Well den,

Hantel, as I said, you must help me perfect my recipes und maybe make up some new eins. We must win dis bake-off und get de zehn marks und show everyeins how gut our food is."

"Of course, Grandmama." Hantel leafed through the books on the table. "Let's pick some recipes."

CHAPTER FOUR

The week flew by with Hantel poring through the old woman's cookbooks. Deciding on five different recipes, they made them from the way she had written them down.

"Mmm, nein, dis is too tart." Hantel had tasted the lemon pie.

"Und dis eins too sweet," Gresel said of the berry shortcake.

"Und dis eins too bland," Grandmama added.

After making some changes to each, adding sugar here, spices there, cinnamon, vanilla or cloves, and cutting back on the lard, they finally had five recipes they were happy with.

Grandmama had tears of joy as she sampled her raspberry chiffon pie. "Oh, ja." She sniffed. "Dis is gut, so gut, und smood und creamy."

"Und dis apple pie is nice und high wid dick layers of apples." Gresel savoured the sugarladen pie.

Hantel tapped his spoon against his chin and thought about the glacè orange and chocolate tart. "Is gut," he finally said. "But I do not know if any of dose are wordy of winning. What is everyeins else's like? What do dey win wid?" he asked.

She frowned. She couldn't tell them that none of them had ever won before because she always put a spell on her cake, so that all of the judges always chose hers no matter how bad it may have been, or how good the others *might* have been.

"Oh," she said. "Dey do dings like biscuits und shortbread, or very plain mince pies. Nodding fancy as dis."

"Well den," Hantel sampled the other pies, "we will beat dem all und win wid eins of dese. Now, which eins should we pick?"

*****

By the day of the bake-off, they had decided on the apple pie and made four of them to entice the judges. Grandmama brushed her hair and placed it into a neat bun, and put on her prettiest dress; a blue floral, ankle length creation that skimmed the ground when she walked.

Hantel and Gresel dressed in what they believed were their clothes, but which in fact belonged to the children that Grandmama had eaten.

After loading the pies into baskets, they hitched up the horse to the cart and made off for Strudelbaker Falls and the Strudelbaker Falls monthly bake-off.

And, of course, Strudelbaker Falls was in the opposite direction to Meringue Ville where the children were from. Grandmama would never take them back to the town they disappeared from. Why, what would happen if someone recognised them and called the police? Grandmama would have to use her powers on the town's people and turn them all into rats and the other children into stew.

Nein, I would never take dese kinder into town. Dey are special, unlike all de odders dat I have turned into food. Nein, dese zwei, especially de boy, know about cooking und could help me win de bake-off. Help me win widout using my powers, dat is. Und if we win dis bake-off, imagine all de odders we could win. We could go town to town around Rheineland und win all of de cooking competitions we enter. We would be famous. We would be de best bakers und dessert makers in town. Hunderts of inns will want our food on deir menus. We would be de most famous chefs in de world...

"Grandmama," Gresel said from beside the old woman. "What will we do if someding happens to you?"

The old woman was puzzled after coming out of her reverie. "What do you mean, Kind?"

"Well, you're old und we're zehn, what happens to us if you die?" Gresel fearfully gripped her by the arm.

The old woman cackled. "Nodding will happen to me for a long, long time. I have been dis age for many, many years."

"What do you mean?" Hantel asked from the other side.

"Oh, nodding," the woman said, slapping the reins to make the horse go faster. "I have been around for many, many years, und will be around for many, many years more. You do not need to worry. You will be old yourselves before anyding happens to me."

Those comments left Hantel and Gresel puzzled, and they exchanged glances behind the woman's back as they came to the outskirts of Strudelbaker Falls.

"It is so pretty." Gresel smiled as she looked around and clutched her doll close.

Hantel sniffed the air that was full of delicious aromas. "Mmm, gut."

Strudelbaker Falls was a pretty little Rheineland town, nestled in green spruce trees with mountain views on one side, and lake views on the other. The cute little handmade houses and stores lined the dirt road, and as they passed through, they saw the Strudelbaker Falls Bake-Off banner strung across the street at the other end. There was a platform with a long table, and people already milling about.

Grandmama pulled the cart over and they piled out and tethered the horse to the closest post.

"Grab de baskets, kinder, we must get our pies on stage."

They gathered their baskets and made their way over to the platform where the other women were waiting to lay out their baked goods.

"Ladies und gentlemen," a man called out from side of stage. "All of dose who are entering de Strudelbaker Falls Bake-Off, please register wid de Post Master on your left, und den come up und place your creation on de table."

Everyone headed for the table at side of stage and lined up to register. All that was needed was the entrant's name and what type of baking they were entering. It all went fairly quickly, and Grandmama laid out one of their apple pies on the table with the note card with her name on it. Once everything was in place, the mayor and judges tasted each baked item until they had gone through all of them.

The twins stood anxiously by Grandmama's side watching from the crowd. The judges gave nothing away, keeping their facial expressions blank as they tasted and sampled, holding plates up to the sun, measuring each cake and pie for width and height to see how much the women could get into their concoctions.

"I wish dey would hurry up," Hantel said. "I need to know if it's gut enough."

"It will be." Grandmama patted his head.

After an excruciating thirty minutes they finally announced a winner when the mayor stood at the front of the stage. "We have decided." The crowd hushed. "Dat de winner is…number achtzehn, de apple pie, by Childa Eta."

"Oh, dat's me," Grandmama gushed in excitement and rushed for the stage. "Oh, danke, danke."

"Mrs Eta, you have a very delicious pie dere, you are very gut at what you do." The mayor shook her hand.

"Danke, danke," she repeated, accepting the zehn marks he gave her. She quickly put them into her small bag and tucked it inside her dress.

"Now, ladies und gentleman," the mayor went on. "All of de contestants can now come up und try deir competition's entries."

Hantel and Gresel raced for the stage and made it to Grandmama's side as she started at number one.

"Mmm, not enough sugar," Hantel muttered and moved to number two. "Not enough salt, not enough cinnamon, too much lard," and on and on he went until he finished with number twenty-two. "Berries not sweet enough." He lay down his fork. "Dere is someding wrong wid all of dem. Dose women should know how to cook basic pies und tarts by now."

"Hush, Hantel," Gresel shushed him. "You'll get into trouble."

"For what?" he replied as they stepped down from the stage. "For stating de obvious? Dere is someding wrong wid all de odder food."

"Well, kinder, let's go und have a nice meal shall we und celebrate our win." Grandmama started leading them off, but a man stopped them.

"Hullo, I could not help but overhear what dis young Kind was saying." The portly man tipped his hat. "I am Frederick Strudelbaker, town newspaper owner, und I heard everyding you said. You are very astute about food." He stared intently at Hantel.

"It's not hard to learn what is missing in cooking, it just takes practice," Hantel replied.

"Ja," Grandmama piped up. "I taught him everyding he knows."

"Ah, und you must be deir Mama," the man said.

Grandmama blushed and waved her hanky in front of her face. "Oh, how you flatter me so, but nein, I am deir Grandmama."

"Ah, den you must know a lot about cooking to pass it on to your grandkinder?"

"Ja," Grandmama replied. "A lot, ja, ja. Many, many, many years of practice."

"Und it has rubbed off." The man pulled a piece of paper from his pocket and offered it to Hantel. "Dis is my address und de paper I own. Would you consider a food column? Recipes, cooking tips, maybe even giving us your doughts on different inns about town?"

Grandmama took the paper. "Well, Mister… Strudelbaker. We will give it some dought. But for now, we must go und eat. Ah, would you like eins of my apple pies…"

The man reddened. "Um, ah, well, only if you have eins to spare. I did try de eins in de bake-off, so if you have anodder eins…" He twiddled his thick fingers together in front of him.

"Of course." Grandmama pulled out another pie from the basket. "Still warm und oh so gut." She handed it over with a smile and the aroma followed, straight into Mr Strudelbaker's nostrils. "Homemade wid love und special ingredients."

"Oh…" He reddened further as those ingredients wafted up his nose. "Oh, dat sounds und smells so gut." He backed away. "Danke, danke."

Grandmama nodded. "You're welcome." She took

Gresel's hand as Hantel had hold of the other one. "Come, kinder, let's eat und see what dis town has to offer."

They made their way to the local inn and found seats in the restaurant. Eyeing off the menu, they decided to try the Pork Roast, Beef Bourguignon, and the Shepherd's Pie.

Hantel critically eyed the décor of the small inn and frowned in distaste. "De carpet needs to be replaced, de walls need a paint, und de paintings are horrible." He stared at a painting of a group of men proudly standing around a dead bear that lay at their feet. "So distasteful," he muttered and sighed. "So, Grandmama, what will we do wid de zehn marks?"

"Put it into de pot to save for some new furniture," she replied, patting her hair back into place.

"What about Mr Strudelbaker?" Gresel piped up from behind her raggedy doll who she was feeding a drink to.

"Ja," Hantel replied. "Dat was very interesting asking me to talk about food for de newspaper."

"Und dat is an offer dat will be up to you, Kind," the old woman said as their meals were placed on the table. "If dat is someding you want to do, den do it."

Hantel dug around in his small satchel for his small notebook and a pencil, which he laid on the table next to his plate. He eyed the meal, looking at it from the right then left. He picked up the plate and lifted it to the lights for a closer look. He placed it down, picked up his fork, and tested some of the beef. He gazed up at the ceiling while chewing much to Gresel and Grandmama's amusement.

After swallowing, he made notes in his book. He tasted the potatoes and vegetables on their own and made notes, then finished off his meal at which point he made more notes. He made notes about the service, the décor, and the decorum of the place. Then came dessert. Not that they needed it as they still had two apple pies in their baskets.

They ordered the Apple Strudel, Strawberry Shortcake, and Lemon Meringue Pie. They tasted some of each and found the lemon too sour, the strawberries too sweet, and the strudel made of too much pastry.

Hantel made more notes and then they paid the bill and left. By now it was afternoon and the sun was heading for the horizon as they clambered aboard their cart and drove home.

"So, what did you dink of de meal?" Hantel asked Gresel and Grandmama.

"De pork was too dry," Grandmama said. "Mine is better."

"De pie was too gristly," Gresel said, clutching her dolly. "Und not very tasty." She pulled a face. "Yuck."

"Ja," Hantel added. "De beef was tough und dere was not much flavour in de gravy." He shook his head. "Why can't de only inn in town have better food?"

"Probably because de chef is a man und can't cook." Grandmama chuckled.

They reached home, put the cart away, and gave

the old horse a quick rubdown, leaving him with plenty of hay for the night.

Once inside, Hantel set to work writing out his thoughts on the inn and its food. After an hour he knew what he wanted to say and neatly wrote it down before putting the paper aside ready to take his review to Mr Strudelbaker the next day. He played with Gresel outside by the stream until dinnertime and read until bedtime.

CHAPTER FIVE

The next day he and Gresel were allowed to take the cart into town to deliver his verdict to Mr Strudelbaker, who stood reading his review with a twinkle in his eye.

"Why, Hantel," he said. "You are a very astute young Kind und have put into words what I have been dinking every time I ate dere. I'm going to publish dis in a few days, on Friday. It will be a regular food column." He dug around in his desk drawer and pulled out zwei marks. "Dis will be your pay every week." He handed it to Hantel whose eyes widened at the sight of the money in his palm. "If you can come in on Wednesday wid your column, we will print it every Friday und you will get paid zwei marks, how does dat sound?" He stared at Hantel who still stared at his palm. "Hantel?"

Gresel nudged him.

Hantel gulped and looked up. "Ja, ja, of course. Every Wednesday for Friday, zwei marks pay." Hantel had never earned money before. For anything. Let alone for writing about something he liked.

"Well den, young kinder." Strudelbaker led them

out of his office and to the front door. "I will see you next Wednesday, und remember, recipes, reviews, ideas und news about food. You are not restricted to just reviewing restaurants. Write about anyding dat has to do wid food." He opened the door. "See you next week."

The twins wandered back to their cart and headed on home.

"Wow, Hantel. Zwei marks," Gresel said from beside him. "You're rich."

Hantel slapped the reins. "Ja, I've never had zwei marks before."

"What will you do wid it?" Gresel hugged her dolly tight.

"Save it," he replied.

"For what?"

"For us."

Gresel stared at him. "What do you mean, for us?"

"For us when we're older," he replied. "We may only be zehn now, but we will need dings as we get older, und eventually move out of Grandmama's when she dies. We will have money."

Gresel blinked. "But dat's just it. We are only zehn."

"Now we are." Hantel looked at her. "But eins day we will be older und need money. So for now, we save."

*****

"Now dat you're earning money you will start paying board," Grandmama said when Hantel showed her the zwei marks. She held her hand out at his shocked expression. "Well, food doesn't buy itself you know. If you want to travel to write your column de horse will need to be looked after und fed." She wiggled her fingers. "Eins mark a week."

Hantel frowned. *I've just gotten my first pay ever und now de woman wants to take half of it away. For what? De fruit comes from de trees so de only food we buy is flour, sugar, salt, etc. Meat is always in abundance, aldough I can never figure out where it comes from, but it's always around.*

Something nagged at the back of his mind. Something about being poor and being sent into the forest for food. *But why would Grandmama send us into de forest? We have everything we need right here.*

Grandmama saw the doubt flicker across his eyes and realised the spell must be wearing off. She relented. "How about you keep it for dis week being your first pay und all, und I will make you my special soup. You can start paying from next week. Sit, sit." She ushered them to the table and bristled about making her vegetable and meat soup, digging out a large lump of freshly frozen eight year old from the cool house out back. The soup took about an hour and she added her magic ingredients before serving. "Dere, get some of dat into ja, it's gut." She placed bowls heaped with meat before them and they hungrily dug in.

Dese kinders are special und I cannot afford to lose dem. De odders don't matter, I needed dem to survive, but dese zwei kinder have to be kept alive for my own use.

After dessert they sat around the fire reading. Hantel read from a book of very grim tales indeed, while Grandmama knitted. Gresel dressed her dolly in a pretty pink nightdress ready for bed.

"When will your review be in de paper?" the woman asked Hantel. Her needles click-clacked away as the wool flew over them.

"On Friday." He looked up. "Mr Strudelbaker wants a column delivered every Wednesday for printing on Friday. It can be about anyding food related. Reviews, recipes, whatever."

"Dat's gut den," Grandmama replied. "Dere's not a lot of towns around, if you reviewed any more we'd have to travel."

"What would be wrong wid dat?" Hantel asked. "We could see de countryside, stay overnacht, do several inns, shops und restaurants over zwei days."

Grandmama thought about it. "We could do dat. Make a nice weekend trip out of it. Dere are some nice little towns alongside de river und drough de forests in de mountains. But I've never been furder dan dat."

"What about de odder way?" Gresel asked.

"What way?" Grandmama stopped knitting.

"Dat way, opposite Strudelbaker Falls." Gresel pointed in the direction of their old home.

Grandmama blinked slowly. "Dere's nodding in

dat direction, just forest. Time for bed." She laid down her needles and ushered the children into their small bedroom.

They were already in their nightgowns, along with Gresel's dolly, and climbed into the double bed they shared with its downy mattress and pillows, and even downier quilt and bedspread. The room was small, consisting of only the bed, a large wardrobe, and a small chest of drawers. Blue curtains framed the little wooden window and matched the pretty blue comforter bedspread.

"Gute Nacht, kinder," the old woman said and closed the door on them.

*****

On Friday, Hantel rode their old horse into Strudelbaker Falls and picked up his two free copies he got as part of his contract. He raced back home, and Grandmama read his column aloud.

"Last Wednesday, I ate in de Strudelbaker Falls Inn. For an inn of such a large size, I expected a larger dining room. A much larger room. It was small und cramped, full of far too many tables und far too many people, particularly drunken men.

We ordered de Shepherd's Pie which was tasteless und gristly, de Pork Roast which was dry und overdone, und de Beef Bourguignon, which consisted of de old fat off de cow, a few scraggly carrots und eins dead potato. De meal was fatty und took forever to chew, und swallowing such rubbish was a chore in itself. De gravy was not gravy. It was water mixed with de remnants of de cooked cow wid nein flavour, nein texture, nein…pizzazz.

We drank lifeless water, und downed tart Lemon Meringue, over-sweetened Strawberry Shortcake, und Apple-Less Strudel.

I don't know who cooks de food at de inn, but dey clearly have nein idea how to cook. Mixing ingredients togedder, drowing it into a pan, und den leaving it in an oven to heat is not cooking. It's killing food.

Food should melt in your moud, be edible und swallowable, und make you want to eat more, make you want to go back again und again.

Dis food made me wish I had never eaten it. De service was mediocre, de inn was less dan. De kitchen should have been looked into by de heald department und shut down by de inspector. Dis is eins place I will never set foot in again. God help anyeins else dat eats dere."

Grandmama looked up from the paper. "Dat's quite a review."

Hantel raised a brow. "A trudful eins."

"Well," she added. "I can't wait to hear everyeins's reaction."

CHAPTER SIX

The following Wednesday, when Hantel rode into town to deliver his second food column, he found Mr Strudelbaker laughing his head off over a letter.

Strudelbaker waved Hantel in when he saw him. "Come in, my Kind, come in. De amount of letters I have received because of your review is hilarious. Listen to dis eins. *Dear Food Critic. Your review of de Strudelbaker Falls Inn was wrong on every level. Our food is superb, our décor homely, und our dining room is exactly de right size for Strudelbaker Falls. How dare you criticise us so. Who do you dink you are? Wolfgang Duck? Signed, Mr und Mrs Boulder.*" He laughed again. "Dey own de place und dey're whinging about de review. Bahahahaha."

"It went down well den." Hantel stood at Strudelbaker's desk.

"Bahahaha, my Kind, it went down ever so well. What do you have for me dis week?" He reached for the paper Hantel handed over.

"Ah, an opinion piece on food, nein review?" He looked up inquiringly.

"I dought I'd do a review every second week

since we will need to travel. We will do weekends away so we can cover several places at de same time."

"Gut, gut, gut idea," Strudelbaker said and handed over the zwei marks. "If you keep dis up you'll get a raise. I'll have your copies waiting for you on Friday."

"Danke." Hantel took his zwei marks and left. Luckily, he was able to go about his business because his name was not used in the column, so it afforded him some privacy. He rode home in silence and told Gresel and Grandmama about the review.

"Apparently de town is in an uproar." He laughed. "I don't know why. I only told de trud about de inn und its food."

"Dat may be, Hantel," Gresel said. "But not everyeins likes to be told dey're not liked."

"Und not everyeins likes being told de trud," Grandmama added. "Dat will be part of dis job. You will tell de trud as you see it, but it won't be de trud to de people running de business. Dey dink dey are de best around, und to know dat someeins dinks dey're not, well." She shrugged. "Dat's not nice to dem."

Hantel frowned in thought. "True. But surely dey must understand dat dey will not please all of de people all of de time?"

"Dey dink dey are pleasing everybody all of de time, because dat is de way dey want it und people should like it or lump it," Grandmama said.

*****

On Friday, while Hantel and Gresel rode into town, Grandmama took care of a few rascally children who came across her house. She was done by the time the twins arrived home and gaily read out Hantel's column, *Pour Some Sugar On It!*

"It has come to my attention dat some women have nein idea how to cook. Dey make pies und cakes und odder manner of dings, but for some reason have nein idea how to eins - measure out ingredients, zwei - decide which ingredients to use, und drei - know how long to bake or cook de guts for.

I was recently at de Strudelbaker Falls baking contest und got to taste all of de concoctions on sample. Most of dem left a lot to be desired, wid ingredients missing, or dere was not enough, or too much of someding, completely ruining what could have been an okay pie.

When measuring out ingredients, start wid less, dat way, if you are new to cooking, or a particular recipe, you can add more on your second try. Always add equal proportions, und write everyding down. Knowing what you put in last time goes a long way to getting it right de next time. Und ladies, cut down on de lard. It is fattening. Instead, add flavours such as cinnamon, cloves or spice.

To make it sweet, add sugar or a substitute like honey. Don't be shy ladies, pour some sugar on it und don't be so bland!"

"Ja, ja," Grandmama agreed. "Some of dem cakes were boring und bland."

"Clearly dey are new to baking und have nein

idea dey can add or subtract ingredients," Hantel replied. "Experiment for gutness sake."

"Where will we be going to eat next?" Gresel asked from her seat beside Hantel on the front porch.

"We could go to Black Forester, de big town way past Strudelbaker Falls. We could take de road past dere und drough de little towns of Applerheine und Lemonville. We can make a weekend of it."

Gresel clapped her hands in excitement. "Dat sounds so gut, can we, can we?"

"I must get a new notebook den," Hantel said. "Und stock up on pencils."

"Den it's set," Grandmama said from her rocking chair.

*****

They packed a bag each and filled a basket with fruit and water, then hitched up the cart and were on their way early Saturday morning. They made good time on the dirt road past Strudelbaker Falls, and made it to Applerheine for morning tea.

They stopped in a quaint looking tea shop, and ordered tea and scones which came with thick Germanland cream and over-sugared homemade jam.

On their way past Lemonville, which they decided they would stop at the following day, they made their way to Black Forester, a town larger than Strudelbaker Falls. They found a lovely inn on the outskirts of town that also had stables for the travellers who had horses and carts, and booked themselves in for two rooms.

Deciding to leave eating in the inn until breakfast, they asked the lady at the desk what sorts of restaurants were in town. There were four, a little eatery, a big burly steak house, a romantic little getaway, and an all-inclusive family restaurant.

They chose the family restaurant and were escorted to a table by the window. Hantel took notice of the décor, service, and cleanliness before their food arrived. Bratwurst Pie, Beef Stew, and Sauerkraut Cakes.

They sampled each and then ordered dessert. Lemon Bars, Caramel Tarts, and Apple Upside Down Cake. Satisfied, they walked back to the inn.

"Well, Hantel, what did you dink?" Grandmama asked, holding on to each one's hand.

"It was gut," he replied. "Not de best, but gut."

"De lemon bars were sour. Why can't anyeins make dem sweet?" Gresel asked.

"Because nein eins can seem to get de ratio right when it comes to lemons," Hantel replied.

They entered the inn and went up to their rooms where Hantel settled down to write up the base of his review. He would add to it later and fix it up into something presentable.

*****

The next morning, they breakfasted at the inn then

set off on their return journey, stopping to water the horse in Lemonville. They lunched in a little family café then set off for home, making it by the time the sun hung low in the distance.

Grandmama pulled the cart up to the small stable out back, and they quickly untethered the horse and brushed him down for the night.

Walking around to the front of the house, they found crushed toadstools, candy missing from the walls, and the mint leaf trees bent and broken. They all stopped in shock.

"Who could have done dis?" Gresel cried out, rooted to the spot.

Grandmama sighed. "Kinder."

"But why?" Gresel asked.

"Candy," Grandmama replied.

"But dat is so wrong," Gresel added.

"Well, you zwei did it once," Grandmama said before realising her mistake. "Come, let's go inside." She unlocked the door and got the children ready for bed.

"I haven't written my review yet," Hantel complained.

"Do it tomorrow," Grandmama said. "I must go und see what else is damaged."

"I will come." Hantel flung back the covers.

"Nein," snapped Grandmama, stopping him in his tracks. "Stay in bed. I will lock de door behind me while I check for damage." She left the room. "Gute Nacht den." The old woman left the house, locking the front door behind her, and with her lantern held high, inspected the wreckage. Candy pulled off walls, toadstools crushed underfoot. She walked around the house and found the damage was limited to the front.

She sighed. "Ah, kinder, dey are such brats. Dey come along und eat my house und trample over everyding like it's deirs to do so." She muttered something under her breath. "Deir parents send dem into de woods for fruit only, so dey will meet deir fate wid me. What is it wid parents dese days? Can't feed deir kinder, so send dem away for someeins else to deal wid." She shook her head. "Namely me. Ah, stupid parents. Stupid, useless parents." She was back in the front yard now, and with a wave of her hand and some muttered words, everything began repairing itself. The toadstools reformed, the mint trees unbent, and the candy grew back on the walls. Once it was finished, she went back inside and locked up for the night.

CHAPTER SEVEN

The next day Hantel wrote up his review, and on Wednesday, rode into town to deliver it to Mr. Strudelbaker.

"My Kind." Strudelbaker clapped him on the back when Hantel entered his office. "Your column is a hit wid de town, und now every odder town wants to know about your little column too. Everyeins is up in arms." He chuckled. "Well, de women are up in arms about being told how to cook." He waved to a big pile of letters on his desk. "All de women in town have written me about dis new man I have reviewing everyeins." His raucous laughter filled the room. "Dey dink I have hired a man to do de reviews. Bahahaha. Little do dey know I haven't." He sat his portly frame down behind his desk. "Und what do you have for me dis week?"

Hantel handed over his paper. "We went to several places. I don't know if you want to print all of it, or space it out."

"May as well take de whole review, my Kind. If odder towns want my paper because of your reviews, den I'd better take what I can get." He pulled out drei marks and handed them over. "You've earned yourself a raise already, Hantel, spend it wisely."

Hantel glowed. Not only from the praise, but from knowing he'd earned a raise in two weeks; a raise he was going to keep from Grandmama.

*****

On Friday they sat on the porch reading out Hantel's new column.

"My little family und I decided to spend a weekend travelling und tasting along de way. We had morning tea in Applerheine, in a quaint little tea shop which served tea und scones wid cream und jam.

De scones, sadly, were dick und dry und did not go down widout de tea. Tea so weak it may have well have been plain hot water as it barely had any tea of any kind in it whatsoever.

De cream was equally dick, beaten to widin an inch of its life until it was barely able to be wiped onto half a scone. De jam was overly sugared, in fact, it was so sweet it will eider rot your teed, or give you de sugar sickness.

We made our way to Black Forester wid de scones still sitting in our stomachs, und dined at eins of vier eateries in town.

It was a familial restaurant, De Familial Rheine, und had a little table by de window. De décor was quaint, de cleanliness not so much, but de staff were polite. We tried de Bratwurst Pie, Beef Stew, und Sauerkraut Cakes.

De pie was dick und juicy, but flavourless und gristly. De stew was nein better, und made me wonder if dey'd used de same cow for bod meals. De sauerkraut cakes were just old. Sauerkraut in cake form. Nein flavour, nein texture, nein style, nein danke!

Dessert was lemon bars, old again und way too sour. Caramel tarts dat left a lot to be desired wid its sugar overload, und apple cakes dat came nowhere near being as gut as mine.

We breakfasted at our inn und encountered eggs not cooked properly, toast dat was burnt, und tea dat was drowned in milk. On our way home we lunched in Lemonville, in its only café, to bread dat had not been allowed to rise properly, meat dat had been left out of de cold box for too long, und water dat looked like de pigs had been sticking deir snout in it.

All in all, our trip was not a gut eins, food-wise. De towns were quaint und de scenery pretty enough, but our food was horrible und de cooks have nein idea how to cook.

God help us, I hope we do not die of sickness."

CHAPTER EIGHT

"Und dat is how we became de world-famous food critics you see before you now," Hantel told the four young children sitting on the floor before him. He sighed, it had been a long one hundred and seventy-five years, although it seemed only half of that had passed, but fulfilling just the same.

"But you were just zehn," a boy said. "Und you became famous."

"Ja," Hantel replied, rocking back and forth in his rocking chair. "We were just zehn, but back den everyeins had to earn a living. Und I always shared Gresel's doughts on de food as well." He smiled at his sister who stood between the children and the front door, listening to her brother tell their tale.

"But how did it start dere, why not de day you won de bake-off?" a little girl in plaits asked.

Hantel nodded. "Ah, you could say dat was de day. After all, it was de day we met Mr. Strudelbaker. But after seeing how popular my column was after zwei reviews, he gave me a raise. Und because odder towns wanted de paper for my reviews, his sales went up und I got anodder raise purely from de trip to Black Forester."

He was old now, with white hair, and a portly well-fed frame from all the cooking and eating for so many years. And while he and Gresel didn't look their age, they were definitely still young on the inside.

"So you got to travel de world?" the older boy asked.

"Ja, ja." Hantel's ice blue eyes twinkled. "We travelled all over Rheineland und into odder countries. We even sailed a boat to England."

"Wow." Four sets of eyes went wide. They were roughly aged eight to ten, starving, obviously, dressed in clothes that had clearly seen better days, and had clearly been sent into the forest by their poor, useless parents.

"What's de rest of de world like?" the older girl asked. Her thin frame had very little meat on it.

Hantel thought for a moment. "Not as rich, not as green, und not as well-fed."

The children laughed, but quickly sobered. "We don't have enough to eat. We're not all well-fed," the boy said.

"Ah, dat's why we fed you," Hantel said. "De dick stew should have stuck meat on your bones, und de candy in de garden should have set off your sweet tood."

"Ja, de candy was yummy," the little girl said. "May we have more?"

Gresel quickly moved to get a tray of candy for the children who all took handfuls of deliciously sweet goodies.

"Eat up, eat up," she said. "We must fatten you up."

The children spent a few moments savouring the sweetness before the boy piped up. "You have lived here all de time?"

"Ja, well…" Hantel paused. The story always was the same. Children would be sent into the woods for fruit, and they would always find their way to the house and always end up staying. "Well, Gresel und I came here when we were zehn. Not long before getting de job as food critics."

"Did your parents die?" a girl asked.

"Nein," Hantel replied. "Dey were poor und sent us into de woods for fruit. Dey kept sending us furder und furder until on de drei day we found de stream und followed it to de house. Dat's when we came across de old woman who fed us und took us in."

The child's eyes widened. "Und you never went home to your Mama und Papa?"

"Nein," Hantel said, sucking on his pipe. "None of de kinder ever do. We were de only eins de old woman kept alive."

"What do you mean…kept alive…?"

"Well…" Hantel blew some smoke rings. "Turns out, de old woman was a witch who ate all de kinder sent into de woods. In fact, dat's why de parents *sent dem* into de woods, because dey were poor und could not afford to keep dem or feed dem. So de only ding to do was send dem off to de old witch in de woods."

Their eyes widened further. "She was a witch?

Why did she not eat you?"

"Because I knew about food und cooking." Hantel puffed some more. "I knew what needed salt, what needed sugar, und how dings should be cooked. She kept us alive so we could help her win de bake-offs around de country."

The children gulped. "What happened to her? Did you kill her?"

"Nein." Hantel smiled widely. "Because she put a spell on de food we ate we believed she was our Grandmama. She took care of us as we grew, und I saved my money for when we were older und would move out. But we did not move out. We were never suspicious of Grandmama until eins nacht when Gresel woke up und heard strange sounds. She went to investigate und saw Grandmama waving her hands around und zwei kinder floating in de air in front of her. She floated dem kinder all de way out back to de cold house und didn't come back into de house for an hour. Gresel told me what she had seen, but I didn't believe her at first. Eins day, when Grandmama was in town, Gresel dragged me into de cold house und we saw a huge pile of meat. I dought it was cow, but den Gresel found jars of eyes und ears und teed. Human teed."

"Ugh," the children cried. "What did you do? Did you kill her?"

"Nein, not den." Hantel puffed his pipe. "Gresel und I talked about it und finally confronted Grandmama about it. Because we were older, und she was weak, she knew her time was coming to an end. So she told us."

"Told you what?"

"Told us about de curse?"

"Ooohhh."

"It would seem old Grandmama, being de little old witch she was, was kept alive only by eating kinder. Now, she did age, but at half de rate of normal humans because de kinder meat affected her, und she took on de energy of de kinder she ate. In essence, she took on deir youd."

"How many kinder did she eat?"

"Over de years…hunderts, possibly tausends."

"Did you kill her? What did you do?"

"Well," Hantel rocked back and forth, "dat's where de problem lies. See, when we found out dat she ate kinder, we asked her why she hadn't eaten us. Und she said because we were special. We also realised dat meant we had parents somewhere, und asked about dem. She told us we had come from Meringue Ville, a place we have since visited to track down our parents. But not long after we had disappeared dey had left town, und after some searching, we found dey had died a few years later."

"Aw, dat's sad," a little girl said.

"Ja," Hantel agreed. "It was. So we had been stuck wid her for funfzehn years at dat time und she was frail, old. Really old." He blew smoke rings. "Und we were angry. Angry dat she had kept us alive, she had drugged us und tricked us und den she said someding dat made me even more angry."

"What was it?"

"She said our parents didn't want us, dat our Mama had sent us into de woods on purpose to be eaten by her. Dat's why, when adults tasted de fruit de kinder brought back from de woods, it was always sour, und dey would send deir kinder back into de woods again until dey didn't come back. Dat's why Mama didn't like de fruit." Hantel's mind wandered back to that day many a decade ago. "She was so angry dat we had come back, und come back wid sour fruit dat tasted so sweet to us." He came back. "She said our Mama und Papa didn't want us, und it made me so angry dat I hit her. She fell into de fire under de cauldron."

He frowned. "It started burning her und she screamed in pain. De smell was horrific. Gresel tried to save her, but I stopped her when de old woman laughed. A cackle dat reverberated around dis very room."

The children shivered as they looked around. They sat in the very room a witch was burnt and killed in.

"She laughed at us und told us we should have let her die of old age instead. I asked her what she meant, und she said, if she'd died of old age de curse would have ended wid her."

Excited murmurs erupted. "Curse! Tell us."

Hantel stopped rocking and leaned forward in his chair. "De curse of de candy house."

Gasps went through the air as the children shivered. "De curse of de candy house?" one repeated.

Hantel went back to rocking in his chair. "Ja, ja," he said lazily. "De curse of de candy house."

"Well…what is it?" a boy cried.

"Well…" Hantel took a few puffs of his pipe. "It seems dat to stay young und stay alive, de witch had to eat kinder. So, she made dis candy house to lure kinder. It worked. She had plenty of kinder to eat. But once we came along dings changed, und den when we confronted her wid what we knew, dings changed again, und it would seem dat if she had stopped eating kinder she would have died of old age. But…" He paused. "Because I had set her on fire, albeit unwittingly, dat meant she was killed by eins of de kinder she took. So dat changed dings."

"How?" the children asked.

"Well…" Hantel laid down his pipe, leaned forward, his arms on his legs, and lowered his voice as he stared at the four young children on the floor before him. They weren't well-fed, but they would have no problem fattening them up as always. "It would seem dat if a Kind she had taken managed in some way to kill her, den de curse of de candy house would be passed onto de Kind who killed her."

"Ooohhh, what does dat mean?"

"Well, it means dat because we killed her, we take on de curse, und de curse is dat any Kind who kills de witch becomes a witch demselves und will need to start eating kinder to stay alive."

Their eyes widened. "You eat kinder? You're a witch?" they ever so innocently and rather naïvely asked.

"Ja," Hantel said. "We killed de witch, so de curse made us witches. Now we lure kinder to our candy house so we have kinder to eat. Tell me kinder, did your Mamas und Papas send you into de forest for fruit?"

Gresel bolted the front door.

MIRROR, MIRROR ON THE WALL

CHAPTER ONE

"Dallas, what are we doing here?" Jett Conway whispered to his best friend Dallas Howard as they met up behind the bushes on Fairfax Street.

"We're meeting Louis, Marchone and Zayne," Dallas whispered back, peering through the bushes for the others.

It was eight o'clock at night and dark as a blackout. Barely any stars shone, and the moon was a mere quarter.

"Why are we here at night…and why are we whispering?" Jett continued, furtively glancing around for an adult that might tell them to go home.

"Because it's not scary enough during the day," Dallas replied. "Quick, duck, someone's coming." He yanked Jett down behind the bushes as three figures slowly made their way down the street. Dallas and Jett peered over the top of the bush and saw it was their friends.

"Psst, we're over here," Dallas whispered.

The three boys sneaked over to their bush and they all huddled down behind it.

"You made it," Dallas said. "Did you bring torches?" Louis, Marchone and Zayne held theirs up. "Good," Dallas continued. "Glad you could make it."

"I nearly didn't," Marchone said. "Ma wanted me to do housework, so I had to race through that and nearly didn't come."

"I didn't want to come coz the thought of doing this is freaking me out," Louis added. "I'm not sure I want to do this, Dallas."

"Do what?" Jett whispered. "You still haven't told me what we're doing, and why we're doing it at night. What are you up to, Dallas?" Jett frowned and punched his best friend in the arm.

Dallas rolled his eyes. "If I'd told you, you wouldn't have come."

"What do you expect?" Jett said, casting another glance around. "We're huddled behind a bush at…" he checked his glow-in-the-dark watch, "at eight-forty at night, *on* a school night. So…?" He looked pointedly at Dallas. "*What are we doing?*"

Dallas looked at each boy individually as he spoke, spacing his words for maximum effect. "We are going to…the old Dolby house at the end of Fairfax!"

Jett's brows flew up. "We're what?"

A huge grin spread across Dallas's face. "We're going to the old Dolby house."

Jett rolled his eyes and sat back on his heels. "Why, in God's name, are we going to the old Dolby house…at night?"

"Ssshhh," Dallas shushed him. "Because it will

be more creepy and freak us out more." He nudged Jett. "Come on, it'll be cool."

"It will be stupid," Jett retorted. He shook his head. "I have no idea why we're doing this, but let's get it over with."

"All right," Dallas crowed softly and the boys quickly, but quietly, took off down the street for the old Dolby house.

Jett checked his watch. Eight-fifty. It was a good thing they were seventeen because at least they could stay out until ten, school night or otherwise.

They made it to the end of the street and came to a stop at the rickety old iron gate at the top of the driveway of Dolby Manor. The moonlight barely made a dint on lighting the place up, so they flicked on their torches as they made their way up the driveway.

The voluptuous trees towered overhead letting no moon through at all, and their torches barely helped light things up as they walked up to the forbidding manor.

They all knew from all the times they'd seen the place in daylight, that the old grey wood was warped and rotting. Windows were broken, the porch bent and buckled. Paint had all but peeled off, and part of the roof had caved in.

They stopped at the rickety old porch steps.

"Whoooo…"

"Ah!" they all cried and jumped back with racing hearts and pounding blood in their ears.

"Whoooo…"

Torches lit up the trees and finally landed on a huge grey owl with large yellow eyes and hooked beak.

"Whoooo…"

"Ugh," came the moans of relief followed by scared, unmanly giggles.

"Come on," Dallas urged quietly.

Five torches shone on the stairs as they made their way carefully up to the porch and across to the door.

Five torches moved back and forth as one across the porch to the left, then the right, before Dallas reached for the knob.

"Whoooo…"

"Ah!" they all cried again, and their hearts took off like wild horses racing down the back stretch of the Kentucky Derby.

Dallas laughed softly, licked his dry lips, wiped his sweaty hand on his jeans, and slowly reached for the knob again. It turned with ease and the door creaked open.

Five torches moved as one to shine through the doorway.

The boys huddled together, glancing around to make sure no one was watching. When they were satisfied there was no one around besides them, they stepped over the threshold and into the dark hall.

Five torches moved as one to the left to see a large empty room with a broken down fireplace.

Five torches moved to the right to see a slightly smaller room with a broken down fireplace and a doorway that led to what looked to be a kitchen.

Five torches moved as one down the hallway before them and up to the stairs to the first landing.

There was nothing. Nothing on the walls, nothing on the floor.

"Let's go that way." Dallas nudged Jett and nodded to the left.

The boys moved into the room, carefully avoiding broken floorboards and holes.

"It's probly the lounge room," Marchone whispered. "With a fireplace that big, and those two big windows…" He flicked his torch across the two bay windows facing the street.

They looked at the bare walls and saw white shapes framed by dirt and dust where paintings and pictures once hung.

They moved through an arched doorway into a smaller room at the back of the house. Rotted wood made holes in the floor, bird nests sat in the fireplace grate. The boards screeched as they moved toward the door leading back to the hallway, and they found themselves between the stairs and the back door.

Sweeping the floor with their lights, they crossed the hallway into what used to be the kitchen. A few rickety old cupboards remained, along with the rusted pipes sticking out of the wall from where the sink would have been under the broken window facing the back yard. Branches and leaves were scattered across the floor, as were bits of rubbish that would have floated in through the windows over time.

Making their way into the dining room, they found bird carcasses in the fire grate and scattered across the floor. Clearly wild animals had made the house their home. They walked back into the hallway.

"We need to go," Jett whispered. His heart had been in his throat the whole time, his blood was speeding around his body, and his gut was tied up in knots he was sure he would not be able to undo. He licked his lips. He was parched, yet his hands sweated, and he'd been wiping them alternately on his pants the whole way round the ground floor. "We need to go," he rasped through dry lips and shone his light near the faces of his friends.

All the boys looked scared, even Dallas, and were whiter than white. Like Casper the ghost after being sucked dry by Dracula. Everyone's pupils were fully dilated, and tongues kept creeping out to lick dry lips.

"Come on," Dallas whispered back, trying not to look frightened, but not succeeding because he held his torch up under his chin and the light detailed every millimetre of fear on his face, highlighted the veins and arteries in his nose, and made his eyes look like empty soulless pools of nothing. "It's not that bad. Let's go check out the first floor." He aimed his torch at the stairs.

Jett glanced at the others. They exchanged frowns, and he could tell they were as unsure as he about going on.

"Come on," Dallas whispered, and the boys reluctantly moved.

They climbed the stairs slowly, trying to avoid rotted steps and warped wood. Making their way to the first floor, they stood on the landing.

Five torches moved as one from left to right. Five rickety doors hung from five rickety door frames at jaunty angles due to rusted hinges and rotted wood.

"This way," Dallas said and moved off to the left. They came across a bathroom that faced the back of the house, with broken tiles and smashed bathtub and sink. Water stains ran down walls, and the roof was rotted above the old shower head.

"Looks like someone's trashed the place," Zayne whispered.

"Probly squatters," Louis whispered back. "Let's get out of here."

They moved to the door across the hall and found a small bedroom deprived of furniture, but not lacking in rubbish and some graffiti.

"Definitely squatters," Louis stated.

A short walk down the hall led them to another small room, and farther on the master and ensuite. Across from that was a smaller room with an old baby's cot, battered, broken and sprawled across the floor in the corner. The mattress lay rotting with its stuffing spilling out. Raggedy white gauzy curtains hung half ripped from the glassless window.

"This is freaky," Marchone whispered. "It's a baby's room. We shouldn't be in here. Let's get out of here." He grabbed at Zayne and Louis to drag them out of the room.

Bang!

"Whoa!" The five of them jumped as one.

"What was that?" Marchone's voice barely made it to a whisper.

They stood in silence waiting to hear footsteps or voices. But there was nothing.

"Could it have been the front door?" Jett whispered.

"Yeah." Dallas cleared his throat. "Just the front door. Let's go check."

With 'are you serious' expressions on their faces, the boys followed Dallas to the landing and he bent down and peered toward the door. It was indeed closed which told them the door had simply slammed shut in the breeze.

"Hello…" Dallas called out. "Anyone there?"

"Ssshhh!" Jett whispered fiercely. "What are you doing, ssshhh."

"Anyone there…helloooooo…" Dallas shrugged at the silence and saw the boy's expressions. "What? There's clearly no one there and it was probly just the wind that made the door shut." He put his torch under his chin. "Let's go check out the attic, mwah-ha-ha." He climbed the smaller, narrower staircase that doubled back on itself up to the attic space.

The boys piled into the room behind him, determined to stay together, and found more rotted, drenched wood, a collapsed roof, and the cold wet breeze coming through the broken windows.

Some rubbish, dirty clothes, and graffiti were in the dry corner behind them, as if maybe someone had been living there at one time, but no more.

"All that's left is the basement," Dallas said,

keeping his voice low. "So far this house has been a bit of a disappointment."

"Weird noises, banging doors, squatters, hardly a disappointment," Jett muttered. "I'm ready to get out of here, how 'bout you boys?" he asked.

The others nodded vigorously in agreement.

"What are you; sooks?" Dallas asked, aiming his torch in their faces, making them blink and look away. "Think of it. We could get an essay for school out of this. Or a book." His head bounced up and down in excitement. "Yeah, a book. About how we braved the Dolby house at night and proved it isn't haunted."

"You don't get rich off writing a book anymore," Louis said. "My aunt barely got anything for her books and she's published several."

Dallas rolled his eyes. "What-ev-ah! We'll be famous then. Problem is, nothing has happened, so we'd have to make it all up."

"Since nothing's happened then, how 'bout we all go home," Zayne said and turned for the door.

"Chicken," Dallas said and started clucking. "Bawk, chicken, bawk, bawk."

Zayne turned back. "I am *not* a chicken Dallas Howard, and if you *don't* stop calling me one I'm going to *punch* you."

Dallas stopped for only a moment. "Chicken, bawk, bawk."

Zayne flew at him with his fist ready to land on Dallas's face, but the others grabbed him, holding him back, and Dallas stumbled back in surprise.

"Calm down, dude," Louis told Zayne as he held onto his arm. Marchone had the other. "Dude's not worth it."

"Yeah," Marchone agreed, looking down at a surprised Dallas who still sat on the floor. "Dallas is just being a *dick*. Ain't you, Dallas?"

Dallas blinked in surprise. "Um, yeah, yeah, just being a dick." He climbed to his feet and brushed himself off. "I didn't mean it."

"Yeah, right." Zayne shrugged off the two boys holding him back. "What-ev-ah!"

Dallas picked up his torch and gave it a shake till it blinked back on. "Let's check out the basement then go. We'll have had enough by then."

"We'd had enough when we got here," Zayne muttered under his breath.

Dallas led the way out of the attic and back down the stairs to the ground floor. Turning left down the hall, they found the basement door at the back of the staircase.

Dallas tried the handle. "Stuck. Help give us a push." He started shoving it with his shoulder. "Give us a hand."

Jett and Louis stood either side of him, and all three put their weight into shoving their shoulders against the door.

"It's coming," Dallas muttered under the strain. The door grated. "It's coming," he repeated before the door flew open and he went tumbling down the stairs. "Ow, ugh, ah, ow, oh, God, ow." Thud.

"Couldn't've happened to a nicer guy," Zayne

muttered dryly.

The others grinned and turned their lights on the stairs. Dallas lay at the bottom.

"Owww…come and help…" he called up to them as he lay sprawled across the floor at the bottom of the steps.

They slowly made their way down and gave him a hand up.

"Ow…I don't think anything is broken," he said, wobbling on his feet before brushing himself off.

"Pity!" Zayne said as he walked past.

They moved around the room, bare dirt floor, old tins, wood crates, spiders and cobwebs, but nothing of interest until they did a circuit and saw something covered by an old tarp.

"Whoa, what's this?" Dallas moved over and yanked at it.

"You don't know—" Jett's cry came to a stop as they saw a couple of big crates unearthed from under the sheet.

"Boxes!" Dallas cried in disgust, kicking at the bottom one. The box on top wobbled and tilted.

"Hey, watch it," Louis yelled, and the boys jumped out of the way as the crates came crashing down.

They waved their arms to clear the dust stirred up by the mess.

"Hey." Dallas coughed. "Look." Four flashlights moved to where Dallas held his. "There's a door," he said.

Zayne sighed. "Another one?" He exchanged eye

rolls with Marchone while Louis and Jett grinned.

"Guys, look, come help." Dallas was trying the knob to get the door open and succeeded as the others reached him.

Another set of stairs led down.

"Cool." Dallas shone his light down the steps. "Let's go."

"Wait, we don't know—" Jett began, but it didn't stop Dallas from descending the new found stairs. Jett sighed. "*Why* does he *never listen*?"

"Because he's a *dick*," Zayne said matter-of-factly. "And *that's* why he shouldn't be left to his own devices." Pushing past the others, he descended as well.

Within moments, all five were at the bottom of the stairs flashing their torches around. It was a small room, maybe half the width of the house, had a hard packed dirt floor, and was now full of disturbed dust that twirled and danced by the light of their torches.

"There." Dallas's light lit upon an object under the stairs and the boys went over for a look. He pulled the dirty old sheet off. "Hey!"

They all moved their flashlights away and covered their eyes, blinking to clear the white spots dancing before them. Their vision cleared, and they came face to face with what had blinded them; a ten foot high by six foot wide mirror in an old gold covered wooden frame.

It casually leaned against the wall and was caked in decades, if not centuries, of dirt and dust.

Dallas moved his torch up and down, back and forth, being careful not to blind everyone. "It's old, there's some damage, horribly dirty." He wiped his hand over the glass, smearing the dirt.

"Ugh, dude, you're gonna be filthy," Louis said, looking around for a rag. He found a piece of tatty white material, probably as old as the mirror, poking out from under the tarp and picked it up. "Here, use this."

Dallas took it and wiped his hand before wiping down the glass.

Keeping their torches pointed down so they didn't get the light reflecting back in their eyes, they studied the old mirror. There were no words, no pictures or clues in the pattern of the wood, nothing to tell them how old it was or who it belonged to.

"I wonder why the tenants didn't take it," Marchone pondered.

"It's huge, maybe they couldn't be bothered," Louis replied.

"Then why bother bringing it all the way down into this sub-basement in the first place?" Zayne said. "It would have taken several people to haul it down to the basement then down here. Why bother if you didn't want it?"

"Maybe they were hiding it," Jett added to the conversation.

Some of the boys scoffed.

"Why would you bother hiding a mirror in a sub-basement?" Zayne swung his torch around. "There's nothing else here. Just that."

Jett shrugged. "I dunno. Maybe it was valuable and they didn't want to lose it in the war or something. This house *is* old and has lived through a lot of bad times."

"Then let's look behind it." Dallas grabbed the side. "Grab it as I tilt it."

"Whoa, careful." Jett frantically grabbed the left side of the huge mirror to stop it from falling. The other boys held it up from the front. "See anything?" Jett asked.

Dallas was shining his light behind the mirror. "Some old ripped brown paper is on the back." He moved the light along the frame on each side. "Can't see anything." He shone it on the bottom. "Mmm, I think there's something down there, but I can't see it. The mirror's in the ground, like it sank or something. Can you pull it out?" He tried to push it forward, but it seemed stuck in place. "It won't move, bugger. Lean it forward more." He made the boys back up so they held the mirror at face height.

They could see over the top to where Dallas pointed his torch.

"Jett, can you see that?" Dallas asked, trying to lean in to see what was at the bottom.

Jett shone his torch on the bottom of the frame. "It looks like a plaque."

"Can you see what's written on it?"

"Nope, you?"

"Nope. Bugger!"

"This thing's heavy." Zayne shifted his hands. "Let's put it back."

"Not yet, I want to know—" Dallas started.

"No, enough!" Zayne snapped and he, Louis and Marchone pushed the mirror back up. Jett helped them lean it against the wall.

"But I didn't—" Dallas muttered.

"Don't care. It's just an old mirror. Time to go home." Zayne said, brushing off his hands.

Dallas sighed. "All right, just let me get some photos." He pulled out the small camera he had hanging around his neck and turned the flash on. He snapped some pics from as many angles as possible as the boys started up the stairs.

When he realised they were gone, Dallas panicked. "Guys? Wait for me." Taking one last shot in front of the mirror, he raced upstairs and shut the door behind him. He didn't bother putting the tarp back on the mirror, nor the crates in front of the door upstairs. And they didn't bother properly closing the basement door on the ground floor, nor the front door as they filed out one by one.

And since none of them had bothered to leave everything exactly how they'd found it, none of them saw the person appear in the mirror.

CHAPTER TWO

The boys met up at lunch the next day at school.

"So, what did you think?" Dallas pulled his camera and tablet out of his bag.

"Of what?" Jett asked, chowing down on his meat pie.

"The old Dolby house." Dallas connected the SD card from the camera to his tablet. "Fun? Weird? Haunted? Not?" he asked.

"Weird," Louis said.

"Freaky," Marchone added, sucking back his soda.

"A waste of time," Zayne replied.

Dallas gave him a filthy look. "You're just a…" He stopped when Zayne balled up his fist and raised his arm, "…party pooper," he finished quietly. He looked down at his tablet. "Let's check out the photos I took." He pulled up the pictures from last night and they all crowded round to look. The house was as it was, as was the basement. Then they saw the pictures of the mirror.

"Man, that thing is old." Louis peered at the tablet upside down.

"Well, if you'd held on a little longer I would have been able to read the plaque at the bottom." Dallas shot him a dirty look, as if to say it was his fault.

Louis shook his head in reply. "Not my fault man. That thing was way too heavy and got heavier by the second. Couldn't hold it anymore."

Dallas scrolled through the rest until he came to the last one. "That's it, I wonder if…" He leaned in to the tablet then enlarged the picture.

"Wonder what?" Jett asked, looking sideways at Dallas. "What's so interesting about that picture?"

"There's someone in it," Dallas finally said.

"What does that mean?" Marchone leaned over Dallas's shoulder. "Someone where?"

"There." Dallas pointed to the mirror. "On the side. There's someone there. Was anyone else in the basement?" he asked the boys.

"Of course not, stupid," Jett said. "Just us, duh!"

"Then why is there someone else in the mirror?" Dallas asked and the boys all leaned in for a look.

"Are you sure?"

"I can't see anything."

"Could be a shadow…"

"Or your over-active imagination…"

Dallas scoffed again. "Not my imagination, dude. My eyes see someone else in that mirror with me."

"And how you gonna prove it?" Zayne sat back in his seat.

Dallas thought about it while the others sat down. He clicked his fingers. "Got it! Come on." He raced for the computer lab with the boys following curiously behind. Barging in, he found the computer science teacher. "Sir, can we use a computer? I swear there's a ghost in this photo and I want to blow it up for a closer look."

Mr Groswold stared at the five boys in surprise. "Ghost? In a photo? Well, I have to see this." Adjusting his glasses, he led the boys to one of the computers and Dallas handed him the SD card. Mr Groswold plugged it into the PC and scrolled to the photo Dallas pointed out.

"There, on the right. It *must* be a ghost."

Groswold stared at the photo on the huge thirty centimetre monitor. "Was there anyone else with you?"

"Nope, just me." Dallas bit his lip. "Is it a girl or a boy?"

Groswold turned a few knobs and pressed a few buttons, zooming in on the section Dallas had pointed to. The machine cleared up the pixels and focussed the image.

"Well? Is that a person or not?" Dallas leaned over Groswold's shoulder and the boys stopped leaning on desks to crowd around for a look.

"Mmm…" Groswold mumbled. "*Looks* like a person. Could be a girl or woman. Someone wearing white…"

The image was clearer than on the tablet, but not as clear as it needed to be to identify whether the form was actually human, and so whether it was young or old.

Groswold printed the image out and they stared

at the picture. "Mmm…" he mumbled again. "Could be a ghost there, Dallas, my boy."

"All right," Dallas crowed and went to high-five Jett who just eyed him with a raised brow. Dallas put his arm down and his grin slid away. "What? I have a ghost in my picture."

"And where did you take this picture?" Groswold asked. "I wouldn't mind seeing the room." He was a bit of a ghost enthusiast, and while he couldn't be sure that Dallas had captured a real ghost in his photo, he was definitely curious about it and wanted to see for himself.

"Uh," Dallas muttered, panicking a bit as they had technically and illegally trespassed on the old Dolby estate. He glanced at the boys with a 'help me' look, but they just stood there with crossed arms and smug looks. "An old estate that we visited…" he finally murmured. "Can't remember which…or where…"

Groswold frowned. "Pity. I would have liked to have checked it out for myself. I'll print another picture." He handed over the one he had to Dallas and printed another for himself. "I'll keep this one and maybe ask some friends of mine that are into this sort of thing."

"Um, sure." Dallas started moving for the door then remembered the SD card. He popped over to the computer and pulled it out. "Better not forget this," he said to the teacher and hastened after the others.

"Great," Zayne muttered when they were outside.

"Groswold's a nutter like you." He looked at Dallas who was studying the photo.

"Yeah," Dallas replied. "But at least he believed that it could have been a ghost, *unlike* you lot."

Jett shrugged. "It's hard to tell anything from a photo. None of us saw anything, but then who's to say the place *isn't* haunted?"

*****

That night, as Dallas lay on his bed, huge headphones on, he gazed at the photo. The pounding of heavy metal drums vibrated in his ears as the slashing guitar riffs sent his brain into overload.

The red bulb in his bedside lamp made the room glow a shade of blood as he flicked back and forth between the pictures on his tablet, which leaned against his legs. His head was propped up on his pillows, and he saw shadows dancing on the ceiling.

His eyes flickered back and forth from the printed photo to the tablet. So engrossed was he, that he did not see the curtains billow gently even though the window was closed and bolted.

The shadows dancing on the ceiling grew larger, and the music in his ears grew louder, harder, more metallic. Yet still his eyes flickered back and forth between the photo and the tablet, trying to see if he could find her, him, it, in any of the other photos he had taken.

He stared from the photo to the tablet back to the photo. At first he was unaware that he, she, it, had moved, as his head was too full of music thumping away in his brain, and the dancing shadows seemed to hypnotise him in the glow of the blood-red sheen in the room.

His gaze flickered back and forth and he, she, it, had moved again. This time he noticed, only slightly, as his brain was too foggy with screaming vocals and slashing guitars. But he noticed nonetheless, that the figure, still indistinguishable, had moved from the right side of the mirror, where only half a person, thing, it, could be seen, to the right so you now saw a whole person, thing, it. It was as if it had taken a step closer to his own reflection, revealing a whole…spirit.

The face was covered by black…it could have been anything if it was there at all. The body was wearing a white dress of some sort with the bottom ripped off. The arms and legs were bare and white and thin.

And the curtains billowed gently even though the window was closed and bolted, the shadows danced fervently, the room glowed a shade of blood, and Dallas's eyes closed against the flood.

CHAPTER THREE

He showed the picture to the others the next day. *"I'm telling you, it moved."*

Zayne guffawed and took a sip of cola. "Are you telling us, you want *us* to believe that that shadow, that thing, that *you* have no idea what it is, moved in that photo?"

"Yes!" Dallas slapped the photo down on their lunch table. "Look." He pointed. "She was on the right yesterday, half hidden by the frame. Now she's in full view. Like she stepped towards me. Now you can see her fully."

"How do you know it's a she?" Marchone asked, staring at the picture.

"I…I…just do." Dallas was puzzled. He wasn't sure how he knew, but it was wearing a white dress so it was a safe bet it was a girl. "Would a boy be wearing a dress?" he asked.

"Back in the old days boys wore nightshirts that looked like nightdresses," Louis pointed out. "It's old-fashioned, but it did happen."

"It's a girl!" Dallas was adamant. *"And she moved.* I…" He stopped, unsure. "I want to go back.

For another look and more photos."

The boys all spoke at the same time.

"Ah no."

"Don't think so."

"Forget it."

Except for Jett who asked, "Why?"

Dallas shrugged. "I dunno. I just know I need to take more photos and to read that damn plaque on the back." He looked at his friends. "Who's coming? We'll go straight after school. Still in daylight. Straight in, take pictures, straight out." He noticed the sour looks they gave him. "Fine! I'll go myself." He'd brought his camera, ready to head off on his own.

Jett sighed. "I'll go. So *you* don't get into trouble."

"Great, meet you at the gates after school."

*****

By the time school let out all four boys were waiting for Dallas.

"You all coming?" he asked, standing before them.

Zayne sighed as Marchone kicked some gravel.

"We need bigger lights, better lights, to really light up the place," Louis said.

"We can stop at my place on the way and get the hurricane lamps, that will help," Dallas said, and led them to the bus.

Forty minutes later they stood on the porch of the old Dolby manor, lighting their lamps.

"Can we get everything ready now, so we're not fumbling with it downstairs?" Louis asked. "Get your camera out now."

"Got it." Dallas hung it around his neck and turned it on, so it was ready at a moment's notice. "Let's go, quickly and efficiently."

They marched as one through the door, down the stairs into the basement, and down into the sub-basement.

The mirror was where they left it, and the four boys stood in front of it holding their lamps up while Dallas ran around shooting photos.

Jett stared at their reflections, lit by the lamps. He watched Louis look everywhere but the mirror. Marchone was watching Dallas, and Zayne stood staring…almost hypnotised, by his reflection. Jett saw a movement on the right side of the mirror as they faced it, between Louis and Marchone. He glanced over his shoulder to see if anyone had followed them down, but saw no one so turned back to the mirror.

There it was again, a slight movement, a patch of white, hovering, moving between Louis and Marchone. A patch of white, white like the dress the person had worn in Dallas's photo. Jett stood transfixed by the barely there figure as it shimmered, but was disturbed by Zayne's whimpering.

"No…mmm…no…" Zayne whimpered, brow furrowed, mouth turned down. "No, no, get away, get away, no." He dropped his lantern and stumbled backward onto the ground. "No," he yelled, climbing to his feet and bolting up the stairs. Jett heard him keep going until the front door slammed.

The boys looked at each other, puzzled.

"What the hell?" Jett said, and he and Dallas turned to look at the mirror to figure out what Zayne had seen. Marchone and Louis turned, but caught themselves and looked away before seeing her.

Full on centre, in her white dress with long thin arms and legs, stood the person, thing, ghost. In one swift movement, her arms reached for the boys as the black thing covering her face parted, and a mouth so large and so full of teeth opened toward them.

Their screams could be heard from the street as they bolted up the stairs and out the door. They didn't stop until the street where they took a breath.

"What the hell was that?" Jett gasped.

"And where the hell is Zayne?" Louis added, clutching both of their lamps.

They looked around, but didn't see him anywhere.

"Call him," Marchone told Louis who pulled out his phone and called…

"Message bank," Louis said.

"He's probly gone home." Jett sighed, regulating his breathing. He checked his watch. "It's nearly five, let's go."

They were silent as they walked, each one lost in his own thoughts and not wanting to express out loud any ideas about what they'd just seen.

I did not just see that, Jett thought. *I have no idea what that was, but I did not just see that.*

Whoa, Dallas thought. *Dude, a ghost. A real live ghost in a mirror.* Once he was home, he plugged his SD card into the computer to look at the photos. Once again, nothing more, nothing less, until he came to the last one. The one he'd taken before Zayne freaked out. He leaned in. "Whoa, dude!"

*****

Jett finished off his homework and glanced at the clock. 10:10 pm. He yawned. "Time for bed." He packed up his books and loaded his bag for the next day. After getting his uniform ready, he went into the bathroom to wash. He was brushing his teeth when he heard his name whispered through the room.

"*Jeeetttt…*"

"Mmm?" He spat out the suds and raised his head. "I'm brushing my teeth," he called, then rinsed off. Standing up, he saw *her* in the mirror. "Bahh!" He stumbled backwards into the shower and slid to the floor.

"*Jeeetttt…*"

She remained in the mirror, staring down at him. The black thing he could only guess was hair was covering her face.

"*Jeeetttt…*"

"No," he mumbled from his position in the shower. "No. You *do not* exist. You are *just* a figment of my imagination. You *do not* exist. *Do not exist!*"

"*Jeeetttt…*"

She faded away.

He waited for a full minute before getting up and staring into the mirror. His breathing calmed, his heart slowed down. *No, just a figment of my imagination. She was never there.* He finished up, left the light on, and went to bed.

CHAPTER FOUR

"You guys seen Zayne?" Dallas asked the next day as he joined the others at their lunch table.

"Nope."

"Nah."

"Not here."

"It's no wonder, if he saw what I think he saw in that mirror." Dallas sat down and pulled out the photo.

"How do you know what he saw?" Jett asked.

"Because I was taking photos remember, and have a load of the photo I took before he freaked out." He slammed the last photo he'd taken down on the table before them, and they peered at it.

In the photo was the four of them in front of the mirror, Louis and Marchone were looking away, Zayne staring straight ahead, and Jett looking to the right. And there in the mirror was she. The she demon, spirit, ghost, whatever she was, in her white dress, with her arms outstretched, and her hair parted to reveal the huge mouth with all its teeth looking at Zayne. And Zayne, the reflection of Zayne, was on fire, burning at a thousand degrees, fire all around him, his mouth wide open, his arms outstretched, his eyes pleading for help.

"Jesus, hail Mary," Marchone muttered, doing a quick cross motion with his hand. "How the hell did you capture that?"

Dallas shook his head. "Dunno. But the questions we should be asking are, where's Zayne, and what the hell is going on with this mirror?"

They were silent for a few moments of contemplation.

"Do you think she can get out of it?" Jett finally asked.

"Out of what?" Louis looked up from the photo.

"Dunno," Dallas said. "If it's a ghost, it could happen."

"Yeah, but we found that mirror and took off the sheet," Marchone said.

"Yeah," mumbled Dallas. He shrugged. "Why?"

"Because…" Jett stared at the picture. "She was in my bathroom last night. In the mirror…*calling my name*…" He finally looked up, an odd expression on his face. A dazed look.

Dallas stared at him. "She what?"

Jett breathed slowly as the others stared at him. "I was brushing my teeth before bed, and someone called my name. I thought it was Mum or Dad and said I was brushing my teeth. When I finished, it called my name again, and I looked up into the mirror and there it was, arms outstretched and mouth open wide like in the photo." He looked down at it. "Just like in the photo…" His voice trailed off and he took a breath. "I stumbled backwards into the shower, and after a few minutes she was gone." He put his head up. "I slept with the light on and took the mirrors down."

The others were silent for a few moments until Dallas spoke. "Whoa," was all he said.

"That's what happens when you stare into that thing." Marchone turned the photo over and stood up. "It gives me the creeps, that's why I didn't look into it."

"Same here," Louis said, leaning his arms on the table.

"So I noticed," Jett replied.

"It's freaky," Louis went on.

"It is," Jett agreed. "It definitely is."

"But you can't think that staring into it makes her jump into your mirror?" Dallas said. "How would she do that?"

"Dunno, but where's Zayne then?" Jett asked, facing Dallas.

"They do say the eyes are the windows to the soul," Marchone butted in. Jett and Dallas glanced at him.

Dallas scoffed. "Are you saying, she somehow jumped into Jett's eyes and went home with him then she what, jumped into his mirror and spoke to him? Don't be ridic!"

"Then how did I see her?" Jett demanded.

Dallas shrugged. "You probly didn't."

Jett rolled his eyes. "Yeah, and Zayne didn't see that..." he turned the photo over, "either, even though you captured it on camera."

Dallas looked from the photo to Jett. "I don't

know," he said earnestly. "All I know is, something weird is going on and we're seeing things we shouldn't be, and now something's happened to Zayne."

"I think we should go round there," Louis said.

"Where?" Jett asked.

"Zayne's," Louis replied. "See him after school."

After some thought, the others agreed.

*****

They took the bus to the stop down the road from Zayne's and walked the rest of the way. It took ten minutes to get to his house, and five minutes for someone to answer the door.

"Oh, boys, it's you," Mrs Blade said. Her eyes were red and puffy.

A cold feeling of dread went through Jett. "What's happened?"

Mrs Blade smiled softly and briefly stepped outside. "Boys, Zayne is in the hospital."

"What!" came four shocked replies.

She put her hand up. "It's okay, we think. When he came home last night he was mumbling about fire and evil ghosts. We thought nothing of it at first, but when he started screaming in the middle of the night that he was on fire and she was going to get him, we called an ambulance and got him to hospital. They sedated him and admitted him to the psyche ward for seventy-two hours." She looked at all four boys. "Do any of you know what he could have been talking about?"

The four of them stared guiltily at each other, not sure if they should say anything let alone if it would be believed.

"Boys?" The inquiring expression on her face told them she knew something was going on.

"Um." Jett licked his lips. "We don't know what's going on, Mrs Blade." Which really was actually the truth. "Maybe he watched a horror movie, or saw something online that gave him nightmares." Jett shoved his sweaty hands into his pockets.

"It was none of that," Mrs Blade announced. "But if you boys can't help, then I hope the hospital can. I'll tell him you came by." She went inside and closed the door.

Jett let out a huge gust of breath and turned away.

"*That* was weird," Dallas whispered. "It's like she knows somehow and was waiting for us to say something."

The boys headed up the drive to the street and made their way back to the bus stop.

"I think we should go back," Dallas said.

"To the Blades' house?" Marchone frowned.

"*No*, back to the *Dolby* house. We need to find out what's going on, maybe even find that plaque and what it says."

"There ain't no way I'm touching that thing with that thing in it, no way, now how, nuh-ah," Marchone stated, waving his arms to emphasise his words.

"*Come on*," Dallas cried. "Something weird is going on. Zayne's been affected, Jett saw her at his house, I saw her move in a picture. Something is weird—"

"And it's weird because *you* wanted to go to that damn house in the first place and took all of us along with you. *You* started this; *you* go back and fix it. Coz there ain't no way *I'm* going back." Marchone flagged the bus down.

Dallas sighed. "Jett? What about you?"

Jett shook his head. "Not really interested in going back."

They got on the bus and flashed their passes, taking their seats as Dallas continued trying to get them on his side. "Louis?"

Louis shook his head. "Count me out. I ain't going near that thing, let alone touching it or staring into it."

Dallas leaned back in his seat. "You lot are a bunch of party poopers. Looks like I'll have to do it myself then!"

CHAPTER FIVE

That night, Dallas spent three hours googling and researching the old Dolby house. He found that it was built in 1835 by Thomas Dolby, and was handed down through the family until the last remaining descendant died in 1985. The house had been rezoned, put up for auction, and had had an attempted demo which had all fallen through or failed. Nobody knew why, they just knew that no one wanted it.

Dallas looked for any photos of the house and family, and came across a website that showed old homes in their prime. The Dolby house was one of them, with Thomas Dolby standing proudly at his front door.

"Definitely not the person in the mirror," Dallas muttered, looking for more photos. When he couldn't find any, he went in search of forums to see if the house registered on any interior design, old homes or even ghost sites. But there was no info there either.

"Clearly no one knows about it." He was so engrossed in the internet he didn't see the shadows dancing on the ceiling by the light of the PC. He didn't see the curtains softly billow even though the window was closed and bolted. And he didn't see his tablet turn on with the picture of the girl in the mirror. He also didn't see her move. The power flickered, his iPod stopped, the computer went hazy.

"Hey, what's going on," he cried, banging on a few keys. He checked the battery. Half full. It wasn't plugged in, neither was the pod, so how, why, and *what* was going on?

He clicked his mouse and banged a few more keys before the screen turned fuzzy, like static on a TV. "Naw! Crap." He sighed and reached for the button to reboot, but his hand stopped just above the button when the screen went black and up popped the first picture of the girl in the mirror.

The tablet blinked, as though it was communicating with the PC, and Dallas sat, fascinated by the picture on the screen.

The person, thing, it, in the mirror, in the picture, moved awkwardly, jerkily, as though it was having its arms and legs pulled by strings. It walked across the mirror, moving, twirling, jerky until it stopped in the background of the mirror, its back to the camera. Its head turned, *it* turned and jerkily ran to the front, banging with both hands on the inside of the glass, trying to smash it, break it, break out of the prison it was in.

Dallas sat transfixed, unmoving, eyes never leaving the screen.

The person, girl, thing, stopped banging and

slowly put its hands to its chest, tilting its head as if to listen. *"Dallaaassss…"*

His eyes went wide and his mouth formed an o.

Its hand reached to the other side. *"Dallaaasssss…"*

He sat transfixed. Not noticing the shadows had stopped dancing on the ceiling and now grew to ferocious sizes with claws and teeth. Didn't notice the curtains billowing even though the window was closed and bolted. Didn't notice the tablet blinking off and on.

The person in the mirror reached out her hands, reached out toward the glass, reached out toward Dallas. Its hair parted in the middle and revealed its mouth. Large, full of teeth and growing larger by the second. It reached out toward the glass, toward Dallas, and this time the glass did not stop it. Its hand continued through the glass of the mirror and made its way to the glass of the computer.

Dallas sat unmoving, transfixed, mesmerized. Shadows threatened, curtains billowed, tablet blinked and the thing's hand extended toward Dallas, toward the glass of the PC, and when it reached it, it continued through the glass of the PC toward Dallas who sat unmoving as the ghost hand came out of his PC toward him. The mouth widened, the teeth grew bigger. The mouth reached the glass of the mirror and kept on going. The arms, the mouth, the head of the thing kept on going, reaching forward, toward Dallas, toward his head.

Shadows threatened.

Curtains billowed.

The thing reached for him, reaching him, fingers right in front of his face. The mouth cried out in a horrific deafening screech. "Mirror, mirror on the wall, who's the deadest of them all?"

The room went black.

*****

Jett lay in bed thinking about Zayne and the picture Dallas had taken. It couldn't be real. It just couldn't. There was no way on mortal earth that a mirror could be haunted and show people weird shit like that when they looked into it. "This isn't Harry Potter's Mirror of Erised," he muttered. "This isn't some kind of kids' story." *What in God's name happened to Zayne? Did looking in the mirror have some weird effect on people? Like the crazy mirrors at the circus or amusement park.* He sighed and tucked an arm behind his head. *Do we owe it to Zayne to find out what's going on? Do we...* He stopped breathing.

The light flickered off and on in his bathroom and blared through the half open door like a neon SOS.

Did he dare move? Did he dare check it out?

It continued flicking, so he worked up enough courage to slide quietly out of bed. His feet hit the carpet and he slowly stood, not wanting to make a sound. Moving one foot in front of the other, he stepped toward the bathroom door. Upon reaching it, he peeked into the room, but saw no one.

His hand snaked inside to turn the light off, but it was already off. He flicked the switch up and down, yet it did nothing. Taking a deep breath, he pushed the door open and stepped into the room.

The cold tiles were a shock to his warm feet, but he kept on moving anyway. He knew the switch was in the off position, so he reached up for the globe thinking it was loose and just needed tightening, but his hands stopped above his head when he saw her, it, the thing, from the mirror, in *his* mirror, standing, reaching, reaching for the glass, for him, reaching out its long white arms toward him. Its hair parted, revealing its big mouth full of bigger teeth and it opened wider and wider. The hands reached toward him, toward the glass, moving through the glass to reach for him, toward him. The huge mouth with the bigger teeth reached the glass, moved through the glass toward him. The mouth followed the hands and reached for him.

Lights flickered.

The thing reached for him, reaching him, fingers right in front of his face. The mouth cried out in a horrific deafening screech. "Mirror, mirror on the wall, who's the deadest of them all?"

The room went black.

*****

Zayne lay wide awake in the psyche ward at the local hospital. The meds hadn't sent him to sleep.

Why would they when he spat them out when the nurse walked out of the room. He didn't want to take them, wasn't *about* the take them and sure as hell wasn't about to sleep. Especially in that place.

He'd been there a day already and that was a day too long. He'd seen three shrinks, been given ten types of meds, and asked why he thought he was on fire. And he'd told them. That he had seen the flames on his body, felt the heat on his skin, felt the flesh burn from his bones, while the stench got into his nose, making him want to retch.

They'd asked him why he thought such things.

He'd told them because he'd seen it in a mirror.

"Which mirror?" they'd asked.

"A haunted one," he'd told them.

They wrote a few things on their paper on their clipboards, gave each other a 'we've got another whack job' look, and walked out the door.

They'd asked his mother questions.

She'd answered the best she could.

"Has he experienced this kind of thing before?"

"No, never."

"Has he been on hallucinogenic drugs for long?"

"Never and I'll sue you if you say that again," she'd said. "My son does not do drugs and a simple blood test will prove it."

They'd given her the same look they'd given him, written something on their paper on their clipboard, and ordered the blood tests.

The blood tests proved her right.

Zayne sighed and gazed out the window and saw

her. Long, thin, white arms reaching for him, reaching the glass, reaching through the glass. The light in the hallway flickered as its hands reached through the glass. The hair parted, and the mouth with the huge teeth reached through the glass following the outstretched arms. It reached for him.

The lights flickered.

The thing reached for him, reaching him, fingers right in front of his face. The mouth cried out in a horrific deafening screech. "Mirror, mirror on the wall, who's the deadest of them all?"

The room went black.

CHAPTER SIX

The four boys sat at their table at lunchtime, whiter than ghosts, their complexions pale and ill-looking. Dallas and Jett had recounted their experiences from the night before, and now questioned whether Zayne might have experienced the same thing.

"It was horrible," Jett said, staring down at his bag on the table as he played with the strap. "I just…" His head moved from left to right and back again, repeating the routine several times. "I don't…" His eyes closed.

"Yeah," Dallas said breathing in deeply and letting it gush out. "Yeah."

"So," Louis started. "Zayne saw himself burning in the mirror, you guys are seeing her in the mirror, but I haven't had any experience yet."

"Neither have I," Marchone added.

"Count your lucky stars," Dallas replied.

"It's because you didn't look in the mirror," Jett said. "The two of you didn't look in the mirror, but we three did."

"So, she's only affecting the three of you?" Louis asked.

"Looks like," Jett replied.

They sat in silence for a while.

"What can we do?" Louis finally said. "Who do we get to help? Who can we turn to for help? Who's going to believe us?"

Jett shrugged. "Mr Groswold?" he said uncertainly.

"My great aunt," Marchone finally said. The others looked at him. "My family comes from Haiti and many people believe in the undead. My great aunt has studied these things for many years. She runs a small herb shop and helps people from my country with their problems."

"What sort of problems?" Dallas was intrigued and had never known these things about Marchone.

"*Spiritual* problems," Marchone stressed the words with raised brows.

"Ahhh." Jett got the implication. "Then we need to go and see your aunt."

"Will she be able to help Zayne?" Louis asked as the bell rang.

"If it is anything to do with spirits haunting people, then possibly. But there are things I'm sure even she cannot deal with."

"We'll go see her after school then," Jett said and the boys went their separate ways.

*****

After school they took the bus to the outskirts of town in an area known for immigrants. There was a large ensemble of different races and cultures and all that they brought to their new home. They got off at the stop and walked a block to a small store, called *Rosa's Spiritual Herbs,* and stepped inside.

The little bell above the door let everyone know there were customers, and those in the shop turned to be surprised by the four teenaged boys in school uniforms.

"Ya," an old grizzled black man said. "Ya bahs a long way from ya paht of town."

The boys stood frozen, but the moment was broken by Marchone's great aunt.

"Marchonie." The portly black woman in a garish floral dress and turban moved through the store. "Pay nah ahttention to mah customahs. Everyone, dis is mah nephew Marchonie." She trundled up to him and enveloped him in a bear hug. "Good to see yah, Marchonie. Ah see ya brought some friends, ya? Come."

She waved for them to follow her through the spicily scented store full of herbs and flowers and other concoctions. "Mahbelle, mind dah store for mah. Ah mah talk to mah nephew and his friends." Leading them into the back room, she shut the door and motioned for them to sit on the couch. When they were seated, she moved a chair in front of them and sat down. "Nah, tell mah, someding is wrong, ya?"

The boys traded glances and waited for Marchone to speak.

"Something is terribly wrong, Aunt Rosa. We have found…" he licked his lips and looked at the boys, "…a spirit."

The large brows on her face went up. "Ah spirit? Tell mah."

With another glance, the four of them took it in turns to tell the story.

"And now Zayne is in the psyche ward for another day," Louis ended.

The woman shook her head. "What have ya gotten yaselves inta? Ya know not ta stir up spirits."

"*We* didn't know when we found the mirror that something weird like this was going to happen," Dallas defended himself.

"Ya, mahbe not," Rosa replied. "But dat's what happens when ya go inta places ya should leave well ahlone." She sighed. "Let mah see what ah can do. Fahst, we must find out ahbout dis house. Who owned it, who died in it, who dat gahl could be."

"Thomas Dolby built it in 1835," Dallas offered. "It's all I could find on the internet."

"Ya, good start. But ah have mah own ways of finding things aht." Rosa heaved to her feet and made a phone call. "Dahril, can ya come ovah now, ah have a job for ya. Thank ya."

"Did she mean Daryl?" Louis whispered to Jett, who shrugged.

"Can't tell what they're saying half the time," Jett replied. That earned him a filthy look from Marchone.

Rosa came back. "Dahril will be here soon, in da meantime, let's look at some books. Come." She led them into a hallway and started running her fingers over the rows of books on the shelves that spanned both walls of the hall.

"We have ta know what kind of spirit we ah dealing wid, so we can deal wid it, ya." She pulled down two books and showed them to the boys. *Spirits Trapped in Objects*, and *Spirits, Time to Go*. "Dese will help get rid of de spirit."

They walked into the back room as a man walked through the back door.

"Hullo dah," the elderly man in black dreadlocks down to his waist said. His yellow Hawaiian shirt blared in the light, and he'd teamed it with white knee-length shorts and tennis shoes. "Hullo Rosa, what can ah do fah ya?" He kissed her on both cheeks.

"Hullo Dahril, dis is mah nephew, Marchonie." She pulled him forward. "He and his friends have ah problem wid ah spirit."

"Nice ta meet ya." The man shook Marchone's hand. "Nah, tell mah ahbout it."

The boys launched into their story again, and when they'd finished, Daryl asked them some questions.

"And where is da house?"

"Fairfax Street."

"And do ya knah anyding ahbout it?"

"Thomas Dolby built it in 1835 and the last descendant died in 1985. And the council hasn't been able to do anything with it since," Dallas said.

"Ah, good. Ah will start thah." He put his pen and notepad away. "Good to see ya, Rosa, Ah'm off ta work." With a nod of his head he left.

They were silent for a few moments.

"Is *that it*?" Dallas finally asked. The boys looked at Rosa.

"Ya, fah now. We must find out infahmation fahst. Fore-warned is fore-warned," she said.

"Doesn't she mean forewarned is forearmed?" Louis whispered to Jett as she ushered them through the store to the front door.

"I think she meant what she meant," Jett whispered back, waiting for Marchone to say goodbye.

"Give us two days," she said. "And do not go inta dat house or anywhere near it." She wagged a finger. "Ya must stay ahway until we can fix dis." She stopped, as if she'd had a thought, and then wandered over to a shelf and pulled small ropes out of a jar. She murmured a few things, waved her hand over them, then presented each one to the boys. "Wear dem, and give one to ya friend. Dey will protect ya from spirits for nah. Wear dem and don't take dem off."

The boys took the braided bracelets and slipped them on. They were leather and some sort of woven material, braided together with beads and crystals.

"Make sure ya friend puts his on and it stays on," Rosa continued as she ushered them out the door. "Come back in two days and we will set up a plan. Goodbah Marchonie. See ya in two days."

The door closed behind them, leaving them standing on the path in the cultural part of town. They fingered the bracelets, wondering if the spell would even work. And what if it didn't? What if that thing in the mirror could actually reach them?

"We can't give Zayne his until he's home." Louis held it in his hand.

"We'll go to his house with you," Marchone said. "We can tell him what's happening."

"Do you think they'll keep him longer than three days?" Dallas asked.

Jett squinted in the sun. "Who knows? Hope not, but if they do, we'll have to break him out."

"Could we do that?" Louis asked, flagging the bus down.

"Dunno," Jett replied. "If he's not home we'll have to find a way to see him."

*****

The next day after school, when they knocked on the Blades' front door, they found he was home.

Louis flew at him, capturing him in a big bear hug. "Dude, you're out. We were worried you wouldn't be allowed home. Jett said we'd have to break you out."

Zayne high-fived everyone. "It's good to be home, but I don't know how long it's for." He led them to his room where they spread out on his bed and the floor. "So, what's been happening?"

The boys launched into everything that had happened the last three days, Zayne's eyes went wide at the stories Dallas and Jett retold, and he told them of his visions.

"It's awful," he said, absently playing with the silver Jesus on a cross pendant around his neck. He kissed it. "Not even Jesus could help me." His family was catholic and heavily so.

"Well." Louis pulled the bracelet from his bag. "Maybe this will help." He handed it over. "Marchone's aunt blessed it or something. Put it on, it might help."

Zayne looked doubtful.

Jett held his arm up, showing his off. "Dude, dunno about the witchcraft thing, but I didn't see her last night. So, no harm in trying it out."

Zayne fingered the brown leather braid before slipping it on. A wave of relief flooded over him, as though a weight was being lifted. He sighed and closed his eyes for a moment.

"Feels different, doesn't it," Jett said from the floor. He was leaning back on his hands watching the change flow over Zayne who sat on his bed. "Feel it?"

Zayne's eyes opened. "Yeah, yeah I do."

"Will you come to the store with us tomorrow? Maybe Aunt Rosa can help you some more?" Marchone asked.

Zayne smiled for the first time in four days. "Yeah, yeah I will."

CHAPTER SEVEN

Since Zayne was having a few days off, they met him at his house after school and then took the bus to Aunt Rosa's shop.

Upon their entering, Rosa's head perked up. Her back was to the door, but she could feel the after-effects of Zayne's ordeal, like a supernatural force barging its way into her shop. She turned and made a beeline for him. "Come, mah child, ah will help ya."

"That's Aunt Rosa," Marchone explained to Zayne's surprise as Rosa led them to her back room.

"Sit, sit. Ah will get ya some tea." She bustled around putting on the kettle and crushing herbs and spices with a mortar and pestle. "Ya, this will help," she muttered as she worked. Within minutes she handed Zayne a cup of hot tea. "Stand, so ah can work." She stood him between the table and the couch so she could walk around him. As he drank the tea, she sprinkled herbed water over him with a small plant branch. Her lips moved, but barely a sound came out of her mouth, and she continued to circle until he'd finished.

"Ya feel betta nah?" she asked, taking the cup and putting everything on the counter.

Zayne thought about it. "I…I do feel better." He nodded. "Yeah, I feel better."

"Good, ya, good. Nah, Dahril is coming any minute, and he will tell ya what he has fahned out, ya. Ya bahs wait here till he comes." She hustled back to the shop and left the boys in the back room.

"Do you really feel better?" Louis asked. "You're not just saying that?"

Zayne shook his head. "Nah, man. I feel better, really."

The boys sat down, but didn't have to wait long for Daryl to arrive.

"Hullo bahs, ha are ya?" Today he had a garish red Hawaiian shirt with blue knee-length shorts. He stopped and looked at Zayne. "Ah, da affected one."

Rosa walked in to see Zayne's brows rise to his hairline. "He not affected anymah, Ah took care of it. Nah Dahril, what da ya have for mah?"

Daryl spread out papers and photos on the table. "Da bloodline of da Dolby family."

The boys eagerly gathered round.

"Start at da beginning," Rosa said.

"Well, Thomas Dolby built da house in 1835 as dis young man said." He pointed to Dallas. "He built it fah his family. He was forty-fahve yahs old and had a wife and two children. He was a plantation owner and grew coffee, wheat and cotton. He'd made his money tha way and could build his own home." He moved to the next page.

"When he was sixty-fahve he died. He was killed bah his daughta, Madeleine." He showed them a picture of the family and Jett, Dallas and Zayne stumbled backwards away from the table.

"Th…th…that's…" Jett pointed.

"Ha."

Jett blinked. "Ha? Oh, you mean her? Yes, yes, that's her."

On the steps of the old Dolby house stood Thomas, his wife, and son and daughter. The daughter had long black hair covering her face, and she wore a white sleeveless cotton dress.

"What happened?" Jett asked. "You said she killed him?"

"Ya," Daryl continued. "In 1835 Madeleine was ten, in 1855 when she killed him, she was thirta. When she was fourteen yahs old she gave bath to a baby gahl. Tha kept tha baby in tha family; let people think Mrs Dolby had had anotha kin. But tha baby was Madeleine's with ha pappy."

The boys all frowned and exchanged glances. "What do you mean *with her pappy*?"

"Biology," Rosa said. "Thomas Dolby got his own daughta pregnant."

The boys screwed up their faces. "Ew," came five replies.

"Tha say Madeleine went loopy." Daryl shuffled some pictures. "All tha yahs of abuse made ha kill her pappy. Here, here's tha family with tha baby when she was ten. Rumour has it, pappy did tha same ta his granddaughta and got ha pregnant too. Tha's why she killed him. He got ha and tha daughta."

The photo was the same as the first. Thomas Dolby standing in front of his house with his wife, daughter and son, but this time there was another girl, just like the first, with long black hair covering her face, and wearing a white sleeveless cotton dress.

"You wouldn't think it to look at them," Louis said. "That he…"

"Nah, ya wouldn't." Rosa fingered the photo.

"Mrs Dolby covered fah ha husband as she covered fah ha daughta," Daryl went on. "She claimed a vagrant had killed ha husband, and said nothing ahbout ha daughta. Nah about tha sixteen year old granddaughta. Nah, in 1875 Mrs Dolby died, and at tha stage she had kept ha daughta and granddaughta, who was fifty and thirty-six respectively, hidden. Tha son, Thomas Dolby junior was fifty-fahve and inherited tha estate and all its problems. He moved his wife and sons into tha house. He had married at thirta and had his fahst kin not long afta. He didn't tolerate his sista much, nah her bastard child, so vanquished them to tha basement where tha sat all day turning inta vegetables. Nah, Madeleine was naht bright ta begin with, and afta what ha pappy did, tha daughta was not bright either. And neither was known to tha son's wife and sons."

He shifted some more papers. "As it turns aht, tha sons soon found tha sister and ha daughta in tha basement, and naht knowing who tha were, or how old tha were due ta tha childlike qualities, soon took advantage and ya had another round of inbred kin."

"Ugh, this is gross," Louis said, clutching his stomach and his mouth.

"Ya, probly too adult for ya ears and brain," Daryl said and continued. "When junior found aht ahbout tha new babies on tha way, he realised what his sons had done, and afta telling them, banished them from Dolby manor. Junior did what he thought was best, and killed tha babies, enraging his sista and niece."

"Who was also his sister," Marchone added quietly.

"Ya," Daryl replied. "Some families are just sick in tha head. In 1880 junior and his wife died, and tha is where it gets weird. Rumour has it, tha sista and ha daughta went mad down in tha basement. Tha had become attached to a mirror that junior had placed down tha, and when he wanted to clear tha clutter tha attacked him. Nah, tha wife had no idea and wanted ta know what was going on, but junior refused to tell ha. Sah, after some consideration, he found a local witch doctor and had him put a spell on his sista and ha kin. Tha spell required tha two to be killed and to live forever in tha mirror tha were so enamoured with as punishment. Junior had tha extra basement dug aht and tha mirror put down tha. Tha wall was bricked up and all was forgotten ahbout until a month afta, when a mysterious disease caught hold of junior and killed him and his wife dead where tha stood." Daryl's eyes twinkled. "Apparently tha maids ran screaming from tha house raving ahbaht long white arms and black hair. Tha's what had killed junior and his wife."

Silence filled the air for five full minutes as everyone digested it all.

"What happened then?" Zayne asked.

"Well, tha two sons came back to claim tha house with tha wives and kin. Tha found tha father's papers in his desk drawer and learned ahbaht tha mirror in tha sub-basement. After finding out who tha girls were, and what tha father had told them, what tha had done disgusted and shamed them both. It was a secret tha would share and take to tha graves. Some forty yahs later. An', of course, all kin inherited tha house until tha last died in 1985, a hundred and fifty yahs after tha house was built."

"You said the wall was bricked up," Jett inquired. "Yet there's a door there now. So *when* was that put in, *who* put it in, and why did no one move the mirror, or say anything about it?"

Daryl shook his head. "Tha is nah mention of it being changed, nah, in any public records of what changes were done. But, everyone in tha family seemed ta die a mysterious death until tha last one was gone."

"What was the daughter's name? The daughter Madeleine had?" Dallas asked.

Daryl checked. "Rebecca."

"So…" Jett wasn't sure of what to say, "…how come…we only see one, and how come, they've said, she said, *'mirror, mirror on the wall, who's the deadest of them all'*. What's her obsession with that, and which one *are* we seeing?"

"It could be ah manifestation of both," Rosa

replied. "If tha were killed and trapped in tha mirror, tha souls may have melded togetha in tha hell that tha exist in. Either way, children, let mah do mah work, and Ah will help ya end this. Go home, rest. Ah will let ya know what we do." She ushered them out of the door, hugging Marchone on the way. "Sweet dreams, Marchonie, sweet dreams, bahs."

CHAPTER EIGHT

A week later Rosa called the boys to her shop. They had decided to spend the weekend at Marchone's to make it easier to go out if they needed to, and now they needed to. They arrived at Rosa's shop at five when she closed, and they all gathered in the back room.

"Nah, mah children. Ah have come up with a plan, but Ah do naht know if it will wahk." She walked around the table moving things as she went. "Ah have read mah spell book and come up with a spell ta stop it in its tracks with luck." She stopped to stare at the boys. "Are ya ready? Ya have ta be ready?"

The boys glanced at each other full of fear, full of dread. But each knew for this to be over, it had to be completely over.

Dallas nodded. "It needs to stop."

"Good, ya. Nah, ya must wear reflective surfaces. Ya need ta wear tha sunglasses with reflective lenses." She handed five pairs of aviator style sunglasses with cords to keep them on their faces.

"We're going to wear sunglasses down into a basement," Jett queried as he checked out his pair.

"It has a reflective surface ta reflect ha advances which is why ya must also wear tha mirrors around ya neck." She handed over small round mirrors on chains.

The boys traded a glance.

"Why?" Dallas asked.

"Ah just told ya, wear reflective surface sah tha evil will be reflected. She gets inta ya eyes and ya soul. Tha glasses will protect ya eyes and tha mirror hangs over ya eighth chakra which is considered ya soul. Reflect ha tha, and she cannot get in. Put them on." She bustled around getting a small box of supplies together; small vials of herbs and powders, and small bottles of clear fluid.

Daryl turned up at the back door. "Hullo Rosa, bahs, ready for tha ghost hunting?" He pushed his own mirrored glasses up onto his head.

The boys said nothing, worried about what would happen.

"Don't worry." Rosa finished packing her box. "Ah will cleanse tha whole house and land. Ah will clean it from top ta bottom." She handed each boy a hurricane lamp. "Nah, let's go and release tha spirits back inta tha world tha come from."

*****

They travelled to the Dolby house via Rosa's minivan where she parked at the gate and got out.

"Let's start at tha beginning." She grabbed a small branch, a bowl, and a vial of liquid from her box. She poured the vial into the bowl and dunked the branch into it. "Follow mah, bahs. Dahril, bring mah box."

From the start of the driveway, she dipped the branch and sprinkled the water, murmuring chants as she went. The boys followed along, each one holding a lamp with Daryl behind them carrying Rosa's box. It was almost like a funeral procession.

Rosa wandered back and forth across the path in a zigzag fashion until she came to the porch steps. She stopped and looked up. "Tha is evil in tha house, ya. Glasses on, bahs, mirrors facing aht, and lamps on. We are going in."

Sprinkling and chanting as she went, she led them through the front door and stepped into the hallway. They took the circuitous route through the lounge and sitting rooms, the kitchen and dining. They chanted and sprinkled up the stairs and into each bed and bathroom, up the stairs to the attic, and back to the ground floor.

They faced the basement door. "Tha is evil in tha," Rosa said in a low voice. "Dahril, mah box." She reloaded the bowl and added a mix of herbs and spices. "Ready, bahs?" They nodded. She turned to the door and sprinkled it with liquid.

The ground shook, shocking them all. Dust floated down from the old wooden ceiling, settling on their heads.

"Earthquake?" Marchone asked.

"Spirits," Rosa replied. "We have a big one, bahs,

be prepared." She turned back to the door and continued sprinkling. "Good spirits come and help protect us. Help us rid tha house and these bahs of tha evil spirits in tha house. Good spirits come and help us."

She opened the door and sprinkled as she went, repeating the verse over and over. The boys followed one by one, holding their lamps high for Rosa to see. Daryl followed up the rear, and they made their way around the back to the sub-basement door. The door above them slammed shut, and the ground rumbled again.

"Whoa." The boys clung to each other as Rosa sprinkled and chanted. The rumbling died down and stopped.

"Good, bahs, cling ta each otha, support each otha," Rosa said, sprinkling the door to the sub-basement. The ground shook more violently and they steadied themselves as dirt tumbled down onto their heads.

"Ya, she is angry," Rosa said. "Very angry." She sprinkled the door and it opened of its own accord. "Ya, she wants us. Make sure ya glasses are on and mirrors facing ahtwards, bahs…and down we go."

Step by step, with Rosa in the lead sprinkling and chanting, they descended into the sub-basement and around to stand in front of the mirror. She was there, waiting, arms outstretched and ready to take.

"Stand in front of tha mirror bahs, heads up, eyes down. Hold tha lamps in front of ya. Do naht look at ha. Look at tha ground."

A hellish screech came from its open mouth, deafening all in the room.

"Ugh," the boys groaned, wanting to grab their ears, but knowing they couldn't let go of their lamps. They hung on.

Rosa sprinkled some liquid on the mirror. "Get back ya unholy beast, get back." The mirror hissed and burned at the water and she went scurrying into the background, hiding behind its hair.

"Dahril, get mah spell book aht." Rosa walked back and forth sprinkling the ground, the mirror, the boys, herself and Daryl. She took the book he offered and turned to a marked page.

She came closer, curious about what was going on in her basement. Screeching softly, "mirror, mirror on the wall."

"That is enough from ya," Rosa spat, flicking the charmed water on the mirror.

"Argh!" She tumbled back. "You have come to kill me." She sped at the glass surface and smashed into it. "You're just like my brother," it screeched.

"Ah," Rosa stopped. "Ya are Madeleine!"

The figure in the middle of the mirror stood silently, its hands on the glass. "You know who I am?"

"Ya are Madeleine Dolby, daughta of Thomas Dolby, brotha of Thomas Dolby junior."

The figure made clicking noises.

"And motha of Rebecca Dolby."

"Argh." Fists flew at the glass; the mouth opened wider, the teeth bared. "Do not mention her to me," it screeched. "She cannot be spoken of."

"Why not?" Rosa challenged. "She is ya daughta, she is ya blood."

"*She* is dead," Madeleine cried hoarsely.

"*She* is ya fatha's daughta," Rosa continued.

"Aahhhh," the mouth wailed as Madeleine weaved back and forth. "What he did to me, what he did to me, and my brother and his kin were no better." She banged her right fist on the glass. "*They* did this to me. *They* created me."

"Ya, tha did," Rosa said. "And Ah am sorry." She sprinkled the glass with water. "But it is time for ya ta go. Ya do naht belong ha anymah."

"No," Madeleine wailed. "No, I will not go. No." The mouth grew larger, the fingernails grew longer and reached back to peel away the long black hair that had covered its face for one hundred plus years to reveal two sets of eyes, melded and moulded together into the grotesque rotted and melted semi bald head of a sideshow freak that belonged to the devil.

Rosa sighed. "Sah, ya have melded togetha."

Clawed hands scratched at the glass, four melted eyes blinked as one. "This is what my kin did to me and that is why I killed them." Madeleine/Rebecca turned her attention to the boys. "Ah, Zayne, Jett, Dallas, you have made my job easier."

The boys all winced, sweating, scared and ready to run. But they knew they had to stand their ground, and hunched up shoulder to shoulder to gain some sense of security and support from each other. They squeezed their eyes shut to keep her out and so they didn't have to look at her.

Madeleine/Rebecca's hand lay on the glass and slowly, surely, went through it, reaching for them.

"Bahs, close ya eyes, but keep ya heads up sah she can't get ta ya." Rosa sprinkled holy water.

"Arkkk." Madeleine/Rebecca retreated then tried again with more force, and managed to crawl halfway out of the mirror reaching for the boys. The ground trembled and its mouth opened. "Mirror, mirror on the wall…who's the deadest of them all?"

"Get back." Rosa sprinkled and chanted in between. "Get back ya evil thing, get back. Oh, good spirits come to take tha evil away."

Madeleine/Rebecca retreated into the mirror at speed and just stood, just watching, as Rosa moved back and forth in front of her, chanting some nonsense. Nails tapped the glass. All five. Thumb to little finger, one at a time, over and over. Her hand lay flat on the mirror, dirty nails tapping away.

"Mirror, mirror on the wall," she screeched. "Who's the deadest of them all? For all the evil has come to play, and now the evil has come to stay, so mirror, mirror on the wall…who will survive this game of thrall?"

The mouth opened showing row upon row of sharp teeth, a pink inside, and a sharp forked tongue snaking its way toward the glass toward them. The tongue stopped just shy of the glass and flicked it as it hissed.

The little ditty gave Rosa an idea. "Stand strong bahs, Dahril, do ya know if thars anything in tha house belonging ta one of them?"

"One of who?" He was hiding behind the boys.

"Anything of Madeleine's or Rebecca's," she said. "Tha must be something of thars." She looked at the melded being that was once human and noticed the torn white dress. "Mah dear, what happened ta ya dress?"

"He ripped it," the creature cried out. "When he attacked me, I fought, he grabbed it and the bottom ripped off." It stared forlornly at Rosa. "My kin did it to me."

"Tha is naht good," Rosa replied.

Louis had been listening intently, and remembered the white cloth he'd told Dallas to use to wipe the mirror the first time they were there. Keeping his eyes down, he slowly opened them and peered around. The rag was a few feet from them on the tarp where Dallas had dumped it. But how to tell Rosa. He was scared to his core, but if it was the torn dress, he had to tell.

"Um," he muttered. Clearing his throat, he kept his eyes down. "Um, Aunt Rosa…" his voice cracked. "There's some white rag over there you could use." He pointed to the tarp.

Rosa saw exactly what he was referring to and kept things casual. "Thank ya, mah child. Ah need some way ta wipe tha dirt off." She trundled over to the rag and picked it up, but the creature knew exactly what it was.

"My dress, that's mine," it shrieked, its arm extending out of the mirror. "Give it to me. He took it from me, give it to me." Its body made it half way out, but stuck, and that gave Rosa the time to duck behind the boys.

She pulled out vials and bottles from her box and sprinkled the rag with all sorts of things, muttering away while Madeleine/Rebecca wailed in the mirror.

"Naht long nah bahs, keep ya courage up." She removed a lighter from the box and walked around in front of the boys. "Come Madeleine, come Rebecca, come for your dress." She held it up in front of her, the lighter hidden in her other hand.

Madeleine/Rebecca reached for it, and just as they took it from Rosa's hand, Rosa swept her other hand up, flicked the lighter on, and set it on fire.

Madeleine/Rebecca shrank back into the mirror with the burning piece of cloth, screeching and wailing as their flesh burned for a second time. For it seemed that setting the bottom of the dress on fire started the rest of the dress they were wearing on fire, and up they went in a writhing, melting, burning mess of teeth and eyes and rotting flesh.

"Naht long nah, bahs." Rosa stepped back behind them and quickly wrote out an incantation for them to say on a piece of paper from her notebook in the box.

The ground rumbled, the house groaned.

"Hold it steady, bahs, nearly tha."

Madeleine/Rebecca's screeching grew louder still, to eardrum bursting proportions. The rumbling grew louder, the groaning grew louder.

They found it hard to stay steady and on their feet.

"Don't look in tha mirror," Rosa reminded them. "Keep ya head up straight, eyes down, mirrors forward, lamps on."

"Arrgghh." Madeleine/Rebecca charged at their glass prison and hand first went flying through the glass. Their body only extended halfway as they once again got stuck at the waist.

"Steady, bahs." Rosa shoved a piece of paper into Zayne's hand as he stood in the middle of the five of them. "Zayne has a piece of paper ya will need ta read from. Keep ya eyes low, ya heads up, and get ready to read from it."

Madeleine/Rebecca clawed for the boys, wailing and screeching about being stuck and why couldn't she come through. The deafening sound was inhuman. She reached for them, her hands, her fingers, her arms all reached. Her mouth, her teeth, her tongue all reached.

"All togetha nah, bahs, say it." Rosa came around to the front standing next to Jett who was on the end.

Madeleine/Rebecca reached, Rosa grinned wildly, the boys chanted in time.

"Mirror, mirror on the wall...who's the bravest of them all, for all the evil can now return, to which they came to now be burned, so mirror, mirror on the wall...this evil will now forever fall."

The stench of burning flesh filled the basement, the screeching echoed to mass proportions. Madeleine/Rebecca reached for the boys, and with a last burst of energy thrust herself forward to within an inch of their faces. "Zayne, come to me…" it cried softly. Almost as if it was seducing him to go to her.

Zayne winced badly, scared of what was about to happen.

"Head up, eyes down," Rosa yelled.

All five did as they were told. They stood straight, clamped their eyes shut, and kept their heads straight.

The ground trembled, the air stank, and Madeleine/Rebecca finally came face to face with herself in five pairs of reflective sunglasses, in five round mirrors, they saw themselves for what they really were. A horrible, repulsive abomination of a monster trapped in a mirror in some sort of psycho witch doctor babble spell.

Four eyes blinked. One mouth opened and screeched the most repulsive sound that had such force it sent the boys stumbling backwards.

"Steady, bahs, repeat tha verse."

"Mirror, mirror on the wall…who's the bravest of them all, for all the evil can now return, to which they came to now be burned, so mirror, mirror on the wall…this evil will now forever fall."

"No," Madeleine/Rebecca screeched as arms flailed and skin rotted. "Nooo…" Its jerky motions made it look like some kind of marionette puppet as it slipped back into the mirror.

"And again," Rosa said.

"Mirror, mirror on the wall…who's the bravest of them all, for all the evil can now return, to which they came to now be burned, so mirror, mirror on the wall…this evil will now forever fall."

Madeleine/Rebecca screamed and wailed and writhed and jerked and flailed, going up in some kind of self-combustible flames that finally made her explode into embers that shattered the mirror into a million itty bitty pieces.

The rumbling stopped. The screeching stopped. All was finally silent.

After a few minutes of Rosa chanting and sprinkling her holy water, she instructed the boys to dig a hole in the ground. She handed them two collapsible shovels from her box, and took out a small brush. "Ah will sweep up tha remains, ya dig tha hole ta bury it."

Everyone set to work, and after half an hour there was a hole big enough for Rosa to brush the broken glass into it plus the chopped up gold wood frame.

"Wait," Dallas cried. "Where's the plaque? There was a plaque on the back of the frame." He grabbed at the pieces and found it nailed to one of them.

"*Do not read it out loud,*" Rosa cut him off. "Let me see it."

He handed it to her and she silently read the engraving. *'To whom it may concern. Do not hang this mirror, do not take it upstairs, do not take it from this room. You will die if you do. It is to stay in the basement until the end of time'.* "Well," Rosa said. "Someone knew ta warn people."

"Didn't do us any good," Zayne said.

"Nah, mah child." Rosa patted him on the shoulder and threw the wood into the hole. "It's nearly ovah. Dahril, mah box." She set about sprinkling herbs and spices, bones, feathers and God knows what else into the hole, chanting the whole time. She poured on salt and lit it all on fire. It burned quickly, but left the air smokey, and everyone pulled their shirts over their mouth and nose.

Rosa quickly mixed her liquids and poured it on top of the fire, dousing it and putting it out. "Tha, now bury it." The boys shovelled the dirt back in the hole and stamped it down when they were done. "It is done," Rosa concluded. "Come, let's leave tha house. It is clean. It is ovah. Tha evil has gone and ya bahs will be fine."

They gathered their lamps, placed everything back in Rosa's box, and made their way up the stairs, closing, locking, and piling the crates back in front of the door. They made their way up to the ground floor, out the door and to their van to see stars twinkling in the sky.

In fact, they twinkled so much it was like they were twinkling all the way down into the sub-basement, amid the ash, smoke, and debris sat twinkling little stars on the dirt floor.

Twinkling little stars in the shape of smashed little glass with twinkling little eyes burning bright within.

The eyes blinked.

They twinkled no more.

THE BONES OF WRATH:
HAUNTED

THE HOUSE

"Hey, Andy, you comin' to my place this arvo?" Damo yelled across the quad at lunchtime.

"Yeah," I yelled back, and pitched my basketball easily through the hoop hanging on the side of the tech building. "Who else is comin'?" I grabbed the ball and bounced it.

"Mark, Jesse, Tyler, a few others," Damo yelled before shoving half a sandwich into his mouth.

"All right, I'll meet you there—" I was cut off by a glare from Mr Neworth who then proceeded to yell out across the quad.

"No shouting across the quad!" When he saw us laughing, he realised what he'd done and blushed. Yep, a grown man blushed. Adjusting his tie, he quickly walked away.

*****

I had to go and get new cleats for soccer after school with Mum, so I didn't turn up to Damo's until five. "I'm here," I yelled as I walked through the open garage into the backyard. There was a game of cricket going on and I took a seat on the porch to watch.

Jesse bowled the ball at Mark and got him out when the ball hit the stumps.

"He's out," Damo yelled, holding up his arms and rushing over to me. "Wanna go, Andy?"

"No, thanks, I'll just sit here and watch."

"None of you will sit here and watch. You'll break a window with the way you're playing, so get down to the oval at the end of the road and be home by eight." Damo's mother, Mrs Benton, stood on the porch behind me with her hands on her hips. "I don't want you breaking anything, so skedaddle."

We grabbed the wickets, bats and ball, and hightailed it down the street to the oval.

"Hey, Damo, I thought that lot was empty?" Jesse piped up from the middle of the pack as we all did a fast pace down the street.

"What lot?" Damo looked around.

"That lot," Jesse replied, somehow bringing us to a halt.

There were ten of us in total, and we all stopped in the middle of the road to look at the last lot on the street.

Lot 666.

It's at the end of a cul-de-sac, or court. The last house lot before the huge oval where we all played after school most days. The lot had been flat and empty for years, or at least it had looked that way. We'd investigated the site before. The whole place was weird. We'd found a few headstones off to the side, and nothing but a foundation where a house had once stood. A lot of overgrown ivy and weeds had control of the land the last time we'd passed it. That was…I counted on my fingers…last week.

Now, there were ruins. Rickety old ruins, like a house had been there and then collapsed in on itself and all that was left was the ruins of the ground floor. Ivy crawled across the walls and down the half-standing pillars on the front porch.

"But…" Damo frowned.

"Wasn't that lot empty when we explored it?" Tyler piped up.

We all stood there, transfixed by the now-built ruins.

"But it was…" Damo added.

"Empty!" Jesse finished.

"And now…" Damo muttered.

"Built," Tony replied.

A bone cold chill ran down my spine. "Guys, this is weird." I wiped my mouth. "And creepy."

"Cool!" Damo cried. "Let's check it out." He ran towards the newly-existing ruins and was on the front porch before any of us could move.

"Damo!"

"I don't think—"

"Not cool man!"

"This is way too weird for me…"

"Come on, guys," Damo called, waving us over. "Come and check it out."

The rest of us glanced at each other. We were all wide-eyed and sweaty palmed.

I let out a whoosh of air. "Okay, we move together as a group. No one wanders off on his own; we stick together." I got silent nods in return, and we slowly moved as one towards the path that led to the house.

Damo had disappeared and we couldn't see him anymore. The lot was deep; we knew it reached far back to the woods behind it as it was the biggest plot of land on the street.

As one, we moved up the path towards the ruins. All the while our eyes darted around, looking for signs of life, besides Damo that was.

"Ca, ca, ca…"

As one, we ducked, looking up toward the tree tops to see a lone crow flapping its way to another tree. It perched and balefully stared down at us while we fearfully stared back.

"Oh," I breathed. "Just a crow."

We relaxed, and rose as one.

"Damo," I called. "Where are you?"

As one, we moved for the porch and I poked the first step with my toe.

It creaked, but remained stable.

As one, we ascended the stairs and stopped on the porch in front of the one remaining door that hung crookedly by its hinges.

"Damo," I yelled. A panicked clenching rose from the pit of my stomach to my throat. "Damo!"

"Boo!" he yelled, jumping out from behind the door.

"Ah!" we cried, and rushed back down the stairs to stop halfway down the path.

"Bahahahaha." Damo doubled over in laughter. "Scaredy cats," he gasped. "Gotchya! Bahahaha!"

"Not funny!" Jesse angrily spat. "This place is creepy, Damo."

"But there's nothing here," Damo defended himself. "Yeah, the house is suddenly here and you can see the layout of the rooms, but there's nothing *else* here. No ghosts, no bats, no Dracula. Come on, come and have a look." He ran back inside, and after glancing at each other, we moved as one back up the path, back up the stairs, across the porch, and through the doorway.

Finally, we stood in the middle of the ruins.

"Look, it looks like the lounge room was here," Damo called as he ran from space to space. "And this was probably the toilet."

I glanced around in the setting sun, watching streaks of colour burn across the broken wood. The wind whipped up and rustled the leaves at our feet, and I shivered despite myself. It was cold, colder than it had been out on the street, even out on the path. The wind created little whirlygigs of leaves and rotted vegetation that danced in the air as the breeze carried them away.

"I don't like it here, it's creepy," Tyler piped up.

I watched him rub his arms trying to get rid of the goose bumps that had arisen.

"Creepy, but cool." Damo stopped in front of us. "This place wasn't here before, so where'd it come from?" He looked around and I found my eyes wandering over the wreck of a building.

"I don't know, but I don't like it either," I said. "Let's go."

All of us but Damo moved, turning, rushing back to the middle of the road where we'd once stood. It was warmer, less creepy. Damo reluctantly followed.

I glanced at my watch in the dying sun before moving my attention back to the house and a disappointed Damo who now stood in front of me. "I need to get home. I think we all do."

"Yep."

"Yep."

"Gotta get home."

"But…" Damo frowned.

"You can come back another time and check it out," I told him. "But I'm going home."

As one, we moved down the street before dispersing at Damo's.

*****

Damo didn't get the chance to go back and check the house out for another week, when we were all back at his house playing cricket and got booted out to go down the road to the oval again.

Curiosity was getting the better of all of us, and we stopped in front of the lot.

Lot 666.

And stared.

Astounded.

Gobsmacked.

Confused.

A first, second, and part of a third storey now stood in place.

"But…" Damo frowned.

"Those extra floors were not there when we explored it," Tyler piped up.

"But it was…" Damo added.

"Not even a bottom floor," Jesse finished.

"And now…" Damo muttered.

"Built," Tony replied.

A bone cold chill ran down my spine. "Guys, this is weird." I wiped my mouth. "And creepy."

"Cool," Damo cried. "Let's check it out." And once again he ran towards the now-existing house and was on the porch before any of us could move.

"Ah, geez, not again!" Jesse muttered. "He's gonna be the death of us."

"Don't even say that," I snapped. "Something must be going on."

"Maybe relatives are rebuilding it? Putting it back together."

"If that's the case they really know how to match up old wood."

"Argh!!!!!"

The sound echoed through the house, wafted down the path, and wandered into our ears.

"Damo," we yelled and bolted up the path, across the porch, and through the now double hanging doors that were in pristine condition.

We skidded to a halt in the enclosed hallway. There were walls and floors and a ceiling of old grey wood. We saw old picture frame stains on the walls, and wear and tear from not being covered in rugs.

"Argh!!!!"

The sound reverberated down the stairs; stairs we bolted up as one. We skidded to a halt on the third floor.

"Damo," I yelled. "Where are you?"

"Argh!!!! Here."

We headed across the space to our right, shifting through mounds of leaves and branches. I glanced up. There was no roof, and the walls were barely waist high. Unfinished, broken, raggedy. Trees towered over those half-built walls, rubbing against one another, creaking, groaning, and making all kinds of weird noises.

I shivered in the cold.

We found Damo half under a pile of leaves and branches, blood running from a cut on his leg.

"What happened to you?" Tyler asked as we cleared the debris away.

"I was running floor to floor when all of a sudden the branch came up through the floor and grabbed my foot. I fell and yelled out," he blubbered. Tears had welled in his eyes, but he was trying to be a manly thirteen-year-old and not shed them.

"It came up through the floor?" I raised a brow at him. "You sure? This place is covered in branches and dead leaves…"

"Well, it wasn't when I came up here." He wiped his face. "The floor was empty and bare, there was… *nothing*. No leaves, no branches, *nothing*. Then all of a sudden, out of the floor came the branch…like a claw." He demonstrated with his hand in a claw shape. "And it grabbed me and dragged me down, tried to drag me through the floor, but I kicked at it and it let go. And then you guys came in and it stopped."

"Sure, Damo," Mark said. "Your leg's bleeding, we'd better get you home." He wrapped a bandana around Damo's leg.

"I'm *telling* you guys, it came up out of the floor and—"

Bang!

We spun around with wide eyes and even wider mouths.

Bang!

"What the?" Damo whispered as we all huddled on the floor around him.

Bang!

"Let's get out of here," Tyler cried.

We grabbed Damo and moved for the door, the stairs, the ground floor, the front door, and finally the road.

We stopped and turned to look. The front door slammed shut with a resounding bang.

*****

A week later we were back in that spot and staring mystified at the now fully built home. The roof was on, there were curtains in all of the windows, smoke gently wafted from the chimney, and there was a rocking chair on the front porch.

All three storeys had ivy wound around them in some way. Choking, controlling, *smothering*. The tree branches scraped against the wood and windows. The grass in the front yard had come back to life and looked high and itchy. And for some reason, we had come back on a Friday afternoon to stand in front of lot 666 once again.

And we were armed with cameras, flashlights, phones, cricket bats, and vivid, but scared, imaginations.

We looked at each other and nodded.

We were going in!

As one, we moved up the path, bats at the ready.

"Ca…awk…ca…awk…" We ducked, looking for the sound. This time, it wasn't one crow; it was a whole murder of crows, flitting down to cover the porch bannister from one side to another. There were so many of them, all lined up on the wood, all looking at us eagerly like they wanted to peck our eyes out.

As one, we moved up the stairs, across the porch, and then stopped. Swallowing hard, Damo and I looked at each other and nodded.

"Awk!"

We jumped, turning to see the crows all facing us. Waiting.

Damo and I reached for the handles…

Eek!

The doors opened of their own volition.

I think I stopped breathing at that point and silently questioned why we were doing this. But then, why did thirteen-year-old boys do anything?

The doors silently stopped against the walls and we stared into the lit hallway. Portraits and paintings covered the walls; rugs were on the floor and staircase. Light filtered through every room, and for some reason, we stepped inside and stopped in the hall.

To our right was the furnished lounge room, fire merrily blazing in the fireplace even though it was the middle of summer. To our left was a dining room. A fully set table was laid out ready for dinner.

Aromas drifted in from the kitchen.

I swallowed hard. "Hello," I croaked.

"Awk!" came from behind us.

We turned as one and saw the crows were now in the doorway staring at us, wanting to eat us.

"Hello," Damo called uneasily. "Anybody home?"

We waited.

"Hello," I yelled. "Is anybody home? We're your neighbours. Is anyone here? Does anyone live here?"

We waited.

Lights flickered above us before going out altogether.

We were in semi-darkness and thanked God for our flashlights.

I flicked mine on and reminded everyone. "We move as one and stay together. Nobody wander off on their own." We all nodded in agreement and moved as one.

In the lounge room, we found a lit pipe in an ashtray beside an easy chair. It was like the occupant had hastily left it there before running off to do something.

In the dining room, we found napkins hastily dumped on plates as if the dinner guests had finished before they'd started and left their napkins to be collected.

In the kitchen, chicken roasted and crackled in the oven, and our mouths watered and our stomachs grumbled for a taste. The preparation dishes sat in the sink waiting to be cleaned.

"Hello, is anyone here?" I yelled again.

We waited.

We moved into the laundry-room-come-toilet at the back of the house and continued moving into the hallway.

As one, we moved up the stairs to the first floor and found four small bedrooms, gaily decorated for two girls and two boys, with frills and rocking horses, where the horses were rocking and the dolls were blinking.

Scared, but determined to continue, we moved as one up to the second floor and found a nursery, bathroom, and a main bedroom with ensuite. The covers were neatly spread back ready for bedtime, and steam lingered in the air from the master bath. But we could see through the open door and there was no one there and no water was running.

"Hello," I yelled again as we walked to the staircase. We stopped to find the crows all sitting on the railing, watching us.

"That's creepy," Mark said. "They followed us up."

As one, we got into a silent battle, eyeing off the crows as they eyed off us. I tried to read their thoughts, wondering what they were planning.

"Do we go up?" Tyler muttered.

"Jesse, have you been taking photos?" I asked.

"Y-yep," he stuttered.

"Is everyone's phone still working?" I added. We all looked.

"Nope."

"Nope."

"Nope."

Crap!

"Our phones aren't working," Mark squeaked. "What if we need to call for help?"

"We'll have to help ourselves," I replied. "Let's go."

We moved to the third floor to find a well-furnished play area to the right, and a lounge and sewing area to the left. We stood in the middle of the room and turned around in a circle to face the staircase.

Squeak, squeak, squeak, squeak.

Ring ding, ding, ding.

Bing bong.

We all jumped at the sounds and turned to our left. The toys were all going. The rocking horse was rocking, the bears were rising to their feet, and the toy cars were zigzagging across the floor.

Brrrrrrr…

"Ah!" we screamed and jumped to our right. The sewing machine was sewing through fabric that moved through itself as the foot pedal went up and down.

Our torches flickered.

"No," Jesse whispered fiercely.

"No, no, no," I added, wetting my pants.

Bang!

"Ah!"

"We need to get out of here," I cried.

"Awk!" The crows sat on the stairs watching us. The bears were coming for us; the rocking horse was facing us and slowing moving forward.

Bang!

"Ah, let's get out of here," Mark yelled.

With the smell of urine strong in the air, we waved our bats at the crows to disperse them and pummelled down the stairs to the second floor.

Bang!

A huge portrait fell off the wall in front of us on the landing.

"Ah!"

Bang! Bang!

The master and nursery doors slammed shut.

"Ah!"

We belted down to the first floor and a vase flew past us, shattering against a wall.

A child's giggle floated through the air…

Bang! Bang! Bang! Bang!

The four bedroom doors slammed shut and then open against the walls.

"Argh!" Damo yelled. "Something touched me." He madly brushed at his shoulder and we could all see the red handprint on his t-shirt before it faded.

"Ugh, this place is super-duper creepy," Tony said. "Let's get out of here."

We turned for the stairs to see the crows waiting for us down on the landing. The curtains fluttered in the window above them even though the window wasn't open. Vines were slithering their way up the bannister and over the walls.

The paintings, lined up ever so neatly on the walls down to the ground floor, fell down with a bang, one by one, in quick succession.

"He, he, he, he," giggled through the house. It grew louder and louder, multiplying in layers to reverberate in our ears. It was like a thousand children were laughing, and it was bouncing off the walls, the roof and floors.

"We gotta get out of here," I yelled in panicked desperation.

Waving our bats and torches, we thumped down the stairs through the cawing crows. Vines grabbed at us, reaching for arms and legs and ankles.

"Argh!" I tripped down the last set of stairs to land with a thud in the hallway.

All of the portraits and paintings flew off the walls and around in circles. The children's giggling grew louder still, competing with the cawing of the crows.

I heard the toys and sewing machine, every door in the house was banging open and closed.

I covered my ears as the others reached me, picking me up as one, and as one, we moved for the open front doors. To freedom. To life away from this maddening hell.

The wind was howling, stirring up leaves and

debris and furnishings, all swirling, twirling, and dancing on the violent tornado of air.

Suddenly, as fast as it had started, it stopped, and everything fell from the air to smash to smithereens on the floor.

We stopped in surprise two steps from the doors, wondering if it was all in our minds.

Bang!

The front doors slammed shut.

SISTER MADLY

"Jessica...Jessica...why won't you come and play with me...?"

I mumbled something intelligible.

"Jessica...Jessica...you said you'd play with me!"

I sat bolt upright in bed, flung back the covers, and turned the bedside light on. I felt so hot and sticky and wet.

"Who was that...? Who was...?" I mumbled dazedly, trying to clear my head of the fog that floated through it. I looked down and found my pyjamas soaked to my skin.

"Blech!" I went into the small bathroom off my bedroom and peeled off my second skin. After towelling down, I rummaged through the closet and pulled on another pair of pjs.

I examined the bed. Soaking wet.

"Blech!" I flung back the covers to let it dry, and settled into the easy chair by my window. The sun was slowly coming up over the horizon and I pushed the curtains aside to watch it. I felt my limbs weaken, felt my lids slowly drift down.

"Jessica, it's time for school. Jessica."

I heard the voice and felt the shake. "What, who…?" I yawned and rubbed my eyes, seeing a blurry image of Mum checking out my bed.

"Nightmare again?" she asked, pulling off the sheets and covers.

"Mmm," I mumbled, laying my head back on the chair to watch.

"It's a school day; you need to get up and get your uniform on."

"Mmm…" I barely managed as I felt sleep enclose once again.

"Jessica!" came sharply, and my eyes flew open.

"Mmm, what?"

"Get dressed for school," she said with an angry expression. "I'll have breakfast ready downstairs."

I scuttled around getting dressed and brushing my hair, so barely managed to make it downstairs just as the toast was getting cold and my brother was finishing off the juice.

*****

"I had that dream again," I told Marcy at lunchtime. We'd been best friends since kindergarten and were still best friends now in tenth grade.

"The one where someone's calling your name?" she inquired before shoving a cupcake into her mouth.

I was always astounded how Marcy could inhale food like a vacuum and still keep her skinny, freckly, red-haired figure. I blinked as the cupcake went down in 0.0002 seconds, and watched her lick her lips then delicately take a sip of juice from her drink bottle.

"Blimey!" I blinked again and looked down at my white bread sandwich. "Um, yeah." I remembered the conversation. "Yeah, where someone's calling out my name. It's always the same. *Jessica, why won't you play with me*? She says it a couple of times, and then gets really nasty and snarls it at me because I don't answer."

"Did you wake up all sweaty again?" Marcy finished off her drink and put the bottle into her bag.

"Yep." I threw the remains of my food back into my lunch box and slammed the lid shut. Suddenly food was making me ill and I didn't like it.

"Your Mum came in to change the sheets?" Marcy clasped her hands together on her lap and crossed her legs in a ladylike way. She faced me and waited.

I felt like I was under a microscope in a shrink's office. "Yeah," I mumbled and glanced away. It was embarrassing to be having nightmares at fifteen, and I'm not even sure what they were about, or who was calling to me.

"Do you have any idea who it is?"

"Nope."

"Do you have any idea why it's happening?"

"Nope." I looked around at the kids in the quad. God, how embarrassing.

The bell rang. Thank God that's over.

*****

"Jessica...Jessica...why won't you come and draw with me?"

"Huh, uh, draw what...? Who are you?"

"Jessica...Jessica...come and draw with me..."

"Uh, okay..." I silently moved the covers back and stood up, shakily at first, then walked over to my desk. I silently withdrew the chair and sat down, then silently pulled out my art pad from the drawer, along with my pens and pencils, and started drawing.

*****

"Jessica...Jessica...what are you doing?"

My hand moved across the page, rubbing crayon this way and that.

"Jessica...wake up...Jessica..."

A hand shook me awake.

"What...what...?" I blinked into the light that now flooded through the window in front of me.

"What have you been doing? Were you... drawing...all...night..."

I glanced up at my mother who still had a hand on my shoulder, just as she bent down towards my desk, a horrified expression on her face.

I glanced down at the desk. Page upon page littered the area with what could only be described as barbaric, terrifying pictures. "Huh?" My brows moved down and my whole face turned into a frown. "What? I don't remember drawing these!" I moved the papers to look at each one. Blood-red crayon, pen, texta, marker, slashed across every page as I saw drawing after drawing of a person stabbing someone who was lying in bed. Red was streaked everywhere, like tiny rivulets dripping from the weapon, the bed, the attacker. It spurted out of the victim. Both had blonde hair.

"Jessica?" Mum said slowly. "What have you done?"

I looked up in horror to see my expression mirrored on her face. "Nuh, nuh, nothing…" I felt sick. My insides were churning in disbelief. I certainly didn't remember getting out of bed to draw. When did that happen? "I…I…" My head moved back and forth. "I didn't…I don't…I…nothing…"

Mum withdrew. "Is it for an art project? Did you draw these for school?" She stood straight, but her eyes never left the drawings.

My head bounced back and forth between her and the drawings. "I…uh…" an idea formed, "…yes… we're…um…studying murders…"

"Oh." She nodded, eyes unblinking and focussed. "That's…good…I suppose…you'd better get dressed."

*****

I told Marcy about it at recess. "It was so freakin' scary. To think, I got up in the middle of the night and made those drawings. I don't get it. The voice asked me to draw with it, and when I wake up, I'm drawing."

"Death, murder, horror." Marcy inhaled a whole banana.

"How the hell do you do that?" I asked, perplexed by her eating.

She shrugged. "Good genes."

I sighed. "All I know is something weird is going on. Maybe the house is haunted?"

"Maybe *you're* haunted," Marcy replied. "It's been known to happen. You need to get a witch doctor and have a séance."

I pulled a face. "I am *not* getting a witch doctor or having a séance. Besides, I wouldn't even know *where* to get a witch doctor."

"I do."

My head spun towards her. "*You* know where to get a witch doctor?"

She shrugged. "Of course."

"Seriously?"

"Well." She rolled her eyes. "A friend of a friend of a friend knows one."

The weight fell from my shoulders and I slumped. "Of course they do!"

✳✳✳✳✳

"Jessica...Jessica...why won't you come and play with me...?"

"Mmmm, nuh...no...go away..."

"Jessica...Jessica..." The voice was louder, closer,

bigger. "*Jessica,*" it snapped. "You need to come and play with me!"

"Who are you and what do you want?" I tossed and turned, not seeing anything, just hearing.

"I, want, you, to, come, and, play, with, me. Now!" it demanded.

"No, no," I struggled. "Go away, leave me alone."

"*I won't go away, I won't leave you alone. I want you to come and play with me.*"

The harsh coldness of the voice scared me and I desperately wanted to wake up. I had to. I needed to.

"Jessica…wake up Jessica."

"No, leave me alone." I lashed out at my enemy, the body-less voice calling to me from beyond.

"Jessica, it's time to get up. You'll be late for school."

"School? School? What?"

My lids slowly rose against the light of the room and I saw my mother standing over me.

"You need to get up and get dressed." She looked closely at me. "Are you okay? You don't look good." She felt my forehead. "There's no temp, but your eyes are red. Maybe you're coming down with something. I'll give you some Panadol with breakfast; that should make you better. Meanwhile, get up and get dressed." She left me to fend for myself.

I rolled out of bed. "Ugh, God…" I clutched my stomach. "What…is…that…ugh…?" I struggled into a sitting position and immediately bent over. "Ugh." I gasped for air and fell to my knees; my head met the carpet and stayed there. I could barely breathe for the pain emanated through my whole entire body.

"Jessica?" my mother's voice wafted up the stairs. "Are you getting ready?"

I took a deep breath and the pain evaporated enough for me to crawl into the bathroom and get ready. It was bearable by the time I made it downstairs for breakfast, and a couple of painkillers made it all but disappear by the time I got to school.

*****

By the time I got home it was pulsating into my back. "Ugh." I stumbled into the kitchen and downed some more painkillers.

"What are you taking them for?"

"My back." I slumped into a chair. "It was my stomach this morning; now my back."

"Which side?" Mum stopped what she was doing to study my face.

"Left," I mumbled as my head rested in my hand before it slipped and I slid onto the kitchen table. "Hurts," I mewed in pain. My eyes were closed, so I didn't see Mum coming up behind me to poke my back and stomach. "Ow." I jumped up groggily. "What are you doing?"

"Hush, it may be your appendix, let me feel."

"Ow, ow, ow, ow…" I squirmed out of her grasp. "I'm going to bed."

"Yes," she said. "And I'll make an appointment with Dr Helfburger for tomorrow. Get you checked out…" trailed up the stairs behind me.

I closed the door, threw myself on the bed and curled into a little ball.

*****

"Jessica…Jessica…why won't you come and play with me…?"

Silence.

"Jessica…" more sternly, *"Jessica…come and play with me…we'll have fun…"*

Silence.

"Jessica," it snapped. *"Wake up and have fun with me!"*

"Ugh," I finally mumbled. "Go way…sick…"

"No, you're not, now get up and play with me."

I felt myself rise from the bed, and stand still for a moment before wafting through the door. I had no control. It felt weird. I felt like rubber. Empty rubber. With no control over my movements.

"Go downstairs, Jessica…into the kitchen…and we'll play…"

I moved into the hallway and down the stairs, through the lounge, the dining, and into the kitchen. I had no idea why I was there. Or what I was doing.

"Go over to the cutlery drawer, Jessica…"

I moved to the drawers in the bench.

"Now open the top drawer…"

I slid the drawer open.

"And take out the biggest knife you can find… and hold it up…"

I rummaged around for the biggest knife I could find and pulled it out, holding it up for the light to glint off its smooth, shiny surface.

"Now I want you to—"

"Jessica!"

I jumped at the loud intrusion, dropped the knife and spun around. "What, what, oh, ah, what!"

My mother was standing there in her pink dressing gown. "What were you doing with that knife?" she demanded.

"Huh," I shook my head. I was so foggy and confused. "Huh, what knife?"

"The one at your feet." Her stern look mirrored her sharp words.

I looked down and saw the biggest knife in the drawer lying at my feet. "Um, ugh," Think Jessica, think. I gulped and tried to think of an excuse. My stomach growled. "Was going to make something to eat. I'm hungry." I avoided my mother's glare by bending down to grab the knife, only to be met with severe pain which I grabbed at. "Ogh." The wind went out of me and I stood. I threw the knife back in the drawer and slammed it shut. "I didn't eat dinner, remember. I'm hungry and was going to make something to eat."

My mother softened. "Of course you didn't. Sit down and I'll make you something."

I sat and watched her flit around the kitchen making me a roast beef sandwich.

"How's your stomach pain? You grabbed at it when you bent over." She slapped the top slice onto the beef, cheese and lettuce.

"Sore," I said, accepting the sandwich and glass of juice. She got more pills from the first aid cabinet.

"I made an appointment to see Dr Helfburger after school. It was the only time I could get you in. So we'll see if it's your appendix or not."

"Ugh," I groaned around a bite of food. "I'll be in pain all day."

"I'll let the nurse know about it, so if you need any painkillers she can administer them. Meanwhile, if you're finished, we'll get you back to bed for some sleep."

*****

Marcy noticed me holding my stomach at recess. "You're *still* in pain?" She pulled a packet of Panadol from her bag. "Here, I brought these in case."

"Ugh." I grabbed the pack and popped two into my mouth, washing them back with juice. "It was bearable this morning, now, it's killing me."

"Is it like, period pain?" Marcy delicately nibbled on a biscuit. "My mother suffers horribly with monthly pain. Apparently, it can get quite bad. To the point you need your bits removed."

I shot her a look. "It's not period pain, believe me."

"You sure?"

"I'm sure," I hissed through clenched teeth. "This is worse than what I go through. Way worse." I doubled over. "I've never felt anything like it. Mum thinks it's my appendix which is why I'm seeing the doctor after school."

"God, why make you wait that long? You're obviously in pain." Marcy neatly placed her rubbish in the bin and closed her lunch box.

"Because that was the only time I could get in."

"Well, let's hope he knows what he's doing, then."

*****

"Yes, yes." Dr Helfburger poked around some more.

"Ow." My body convulsed upward. "That hurt!"

"Yes, yes, it would," he replied. Pulling off his gloves, he threw them into the bin and sat behind his desk. "You can get down now."

I slowly rolled onto my side, pushed myself up into a sitting position, and slid to the floor.

"Well, doctor, is it her appendix?" my mother asked while I slid into the seat beside her.

"Most likely. I'm writing a letter for the hospital. Take her to Mercy General Children's tomorrow and they will do an ultrasound, and if it is the appendix, they will make a time for surgery." He glanced up. "It seems to be rather large, bulging almost. Definitely bigger than I've ever felt. And when they start to bulge they could burst." He scribbled some more. "Her temperature is up and she more than likely has a fever, so give her more Panadol and get her to the hospital tomorrow. She will be fine after surgery." He whipped out an envelope, folded the paper and stuffed it in before handing it over. "It's quite large, so it needs to be checked out."

"Thank you, doctor." Mum stuffed the envelope into her bag and turned to me. "Time to get you home."

She helped me to the car and we headed home where I stayed on the couch. I was fed and watered and given painkillers, and come bedtime, I was helped upstairs and tucked into bed.

Mum sat on the side of the bed and brushed my hair from my eyes. "Hopefully tomorrow this will all be sorted out. Good night." She kissed my forehead.

"Night," I mumbled through hazy eyes. I waited for her to turn off the light and close the door. Flinging back the covers, I pulled up my pj top. Slowly, gently, I ran my hand over my stomach and felt it. The bulge. It wasn't big, but I could feel the rise against the rest of my abdomen. I poked slightly. It was tender and I felt the pain. I poked a bit harder and clenched my jaw. I felt around the lump; felt the outline, the circumference. It wasn't round. It wasn't…anything but odd. It felt odd and weird and…different. I pulled my top down, covered myself, and tried to get some sleep.

*****

"Jessica…Jessica…why won't you come and play with me?"

Silence.

"Jessica…Jessica…I want you to come and play with me…"

Silence.

"Jessica, wake up," it snapped. *"We are going to play!"*

I slowly pushed the covers back and stood. I slowly walked across the room and opened the door. I slowly walked down the stairs and stood in the hallway.

"Go into the kitchen…"

I slowly walked into the kitchen.

"Open the knife drawer…"

I slowly opened the cutlery drawer.

"Pull out the big sharp knife you had before…"

I slowly lifted the knife out and held it up.

"Now pull up your pj top…"

I slowly pulled up my top.

"Now…stab yourself in the abdomen…"

"What?"

"Go ahead…stab yourself…stab that pain and end it all."

"What?"

"Go ahead." The voice escalated into a scream. *"Stab yourself and stop the pain. End it all so I can be free…"*

I slowly turned the knife around so it aimed at me.

"Jessica?" The light flicked on and my head spun to see my parents standing there shocked out of their minds, horrified expressions on their wide-eyed faces.

"I am not Jessica," I snapped. *"I am Elizabeth, and it's my turn to live."* I raised the knife and plunged it into my abdomen, aiming for the pain that now bulged through my stomach, like it was some sort of

alien trying to make its way out through my skin.

"Jessica!" my parents screamed.

"Aaaahhhh!" I screamed, slumping to the floor at the searing heat inflicting itself upon my soul…

Fade to black…

*****

"Doctor, how is she?"

The words came in whispers, floating along on a drug-filled haze…

"She'll survive," came a man's voice. A man not my father.

"What happened to her? Why did she stab herself?"

"Possibly the pain was too much to bear and mixed with an excess of painkillers…"

"I only gave her two—"

"Except she had more than two in her system."

"Then she must have had more. Obviously her appendix was ready to burst and too much for her to bear."

"Her appendix?"

"Yes, that's what our family doctor told us it was. He told us to make an appointment here at the hospital for today to see someone."

"Oh…well, Mrs Blakefield, it wasn't her appendix that was the problem."

"Then…what was it, doctor?"

"That was a dead foetus, Mrs Blakefield."

Silence.

"What?"

"Were you pregnant with twins while having Jessica, Mrs Blakefield?"

Silence.

"Yes."

"And one of them died?"

Silence.

"Yes."

"Yes, normally the baby dies and is removed, but yours was absorbed by your daughter, the healthy twin. The dead twin has lived within her since before birth. It's called Vanishing Twin Syndrome, or VTS."

Silence.

"What?"

"The twin was still inside of you and was absorbed by Jessica, Mrs Blakefield. I removed the foetus from your daughter during surgery."

Silence…

A long silence…

"Jessica?"

My eyes took a while to flitter open.

"Why did you say your name was Elizabeth?"

"I don't know…" slowly came from between my lips. I was groggy and not sure I should have been having this conversation right now. "Who's Elizabeth?"

Mum frowned.

"I heard."

She sighed. "I've never told you, and never said a word about it to you, but when I was pregnant, I was having two of you. You had a sister. A twin sister. But sadly, one didn't make it. We named her Elizabeth."

I smiled softly. "I had a twin."

"Yes, sweetie, you had a twin. I'm so sorry. I didn't know that this had happened to you. I didn't know that…the baby…had been absorbed by you."

"It's okay…" I muttered. "Not your fault."

"I feel like it is though."

"It's not…" I drifted off into my drug-fuelled haze. Silence…

"Jessica…Jessica…why won't you come and play with me…?"

"Hello, Elizabeth."

"Hello, Jessica. Let's go and play shall we?"

23

"Come on, kids, time to wake up, we've made it to the motel."

I felt myself being nudged, and opened my eyes to see we had stopped outside of a huge motel.

"Are we there yet?" my sister, Mel, asked, yawning so wide her jaw cracked. "Ow." She rubbed it.

"Yes, we are," Mum said while Dad slammed the back door of the car.

We climbed out and stood looking at the huge old rickety building before us. It was three storeys of splintering wood, peeling paint, flickering lights, and a vacancy sign that couldn't make up its mind if it wanted to be on or off.

Mum and Dad had promised us a seaside holiday with a stay in a quaint seaside motel with a beach out the back.

I sniffed the air. "Ewww. That's not beach, that's—"

"Seaweed," my sister finished, her brows wrinkling at the horrible smell.

"Andrew," Dad warned. "No complaining now, we're already late in getting here, and they agreed to hold our rooms for us, so grab your bags and let's go."

"Besides..." Mum's smile was half apologetic. "I'm sure it will look better in the morning when you go and explore."

"Ugh." I glanced at Mel and we traded frowns.

Lugging our cases and backpacks through the old screen door, we found ourselves in an old-fashioned, red carpeted, green walled and blue curtained nightmare.

Out of a back door a little old lady tottered in on her cane. "Well, hello there, you must be the Bates family?"

"Yes." Dad stepped forward. "We're so sorry we're late. We got lost and ran out of petrol. We called hoping you could keep our rooms."

"Of course, of course." The brightness of her little grandma voice chirped around the room. "We understand that things can happen. So we try to accommodate our guests."

"Thank you so much," Mum replied. "We'll pay now and head on up."

"Of course," the little old grandma said and quickly took Dad's credit card. A few moments later she was done and called out to someone. "Brutus, can you help the Bates family with their luggage and show them to their room?"

Out of the back door came the biggest, hairiest man I'd ever seen. He was the cartoon style hairy ape caveman, with arms so long his knuckles dragged on the ground. He was unshaven, wearing tatty clothes and muddied shoes. I knew I had seen him in one of those cartoons somewhere.

We gathered our bags and followed him up to the third floor where he parked outside of a door. "Mr and Mrs Bates, you are here."

Mel and I glanced at each other and stifled a giggle. Our eyes were wide at his lisping drawl, and I could swear drool was dripping down the side of his mouth.

"Um." Mum and Dad exchanged a glance. "Thank you." They opened their door and placed their bags inside.

Brutus turned and moved down the hall to the next door. "This is for the rug rats." He waved an arm the thickness of a tree stump, and Mel and I stopped.

I gulped. "Thank you," came out high-pitched and girly like.

"Welcome." Brutus turned and walked down the dark, badly lit hallway with its blood-red carpet and green walls. Looked like the whole motel was decorated the same way.

"Kids, let's get you settled." Mum came up behind us and Mel and I turned to our room.

Number 23.

Mum let us in and flicked on the light. "There's a connecting door between our rooms, so we'll leave that unlocked and open." She fiddled with the lock while we dragged our bags in.

Surprisingly, the room was nicely decorated, and we stopped and stared at the polished wood floor, a light blue wall colour with matching blue and white curtains billowing on the breeze from the open window. The twin beds were covered in blue spreads, and the decorations were nautical in theme.

"Wow," Mel muttered. "This room has a beachy theme. Dibs on the bed by the window." She threw her backpack onto the bed.

"Well, it is a beachside motel," Mum said, opening the door between our rooms and then locking the door to the hallway. "You can leave your unpacking until tomorrow. It's late, so just jump in bed."

I grabbed a brochure from the bedside table and looked at it. The photo on the glossy page did not resemble what I had seen outside. And neither did the interior décor that the brochure also bragged about.

"2323 Old Beachside Way," I read from the page. "And we're in room 23, how's that? Room 23, 2323 Old Beachside Way." I looked up to see Mum gone and Mel pulling on her pjs.

"I'm using the bathroom and then jumping in bed," she said. "You'll have to wait."

I watched her close the door then turned my back to stare out the window into the starry night sky. I leaned out far, listening for the beach and getting crashing waves in return. I scanned the panorama, but saw only bobbing lights, the flickering lighthouse, and the millions of stars above.

"Finished."

I stuck my head back in to see Mel crawling into bed. As twins, we were not one bit alike. Not one bit. But we always had to share. It would be nice, just once, to get my own room on vacations. I used the bathroom and changed into my own pjs before settling into bed.

I waved my phone around. "Ah, bum, no bars. What about you?"

Mel flicked off her tablet. "Internet's awful, cuts in and out." We dumped our tech on the bedside cupboard between us and lay back, listening to the waves crash on the beach.

Thump…

Bang…

Hey, what?

Thump…

Bang…

I sat up to see the wall behind our beds banging away from the other side. Whatever was hitting it, or ramming into it, was so forceful that our bedheads banged back and forth.

"Hey." Mel sat up. "What's going on?"

"Dunno, but I'm gonna go and tell 'em to stop." I flung back the covers and rammed my feet into my slippers. The banging was still happening, but this time my bed was moving away from the wall with every bang.

"We should tell Mum and Dad, we can't do this ourselves." Mel was now beside me.

"It's only the next room over, it won't take long." I unlocked the door and stuck my head into the hallway. The lights lazily flickered, but other than that, there wasn't much else happening.

Leaving the door wide open, we tiptoed next door, to number 25, and firmly knocked on the door.

Silence.

"Go back and see if they've stopped," I told Mel, and watched her silently run back to our room and stick her head through the door.

"I don't hear anything," she whispered loudly, running back to me. "Maybe they freaked out when you knocked?" She grasped my arm. "Let's go."

"No." I knocked again and listened. There was no sound of any kind coming from behind the door, so I tried the handle. Locked.

"*Of course* it would be locked, silly," Mel chastised. "There are people staying in there."

"Yeah," I muttered. "You're right. Let's go back to bed." We walked back into our room and the door slammed shut behind us.

It was not our room.

"Wait, isn't this our room?" I was confused. We had just walked back into our room, yet it was not our room. The décor, furnishings, everything was different. It had retro, old-style decor. "This is definitely not our room," I stated.

"Andy, there's no door to Mum and Dad's room." Mel stood looking at the wall to the right of the door and there was definitely no connecting door there.

"Wait, no, let's check the number on the door." I opened the door and we walked into the hallway. Same red carpet, same green paint. We looked at the door number across from us. 22. We walked down to Mum and Dad's. 21. We walked back to ours and noticed the door had closed, but still, it read 23.

Mel and I looked at each other, perplexed by the situation. I grasped the handle and turned, pushing it open. We stepped inside and found ourselves back in the hallway.

"What? Wait, what just happened?" Mel asked from beside me. "Didn't we just go into our room?"

I looked to my left and saw our door was closed.

"Hey, excuse me," I heard Mel call and turned. At the end of the hallway stood a white-haired boy that looked to be about our age.

"Who's that?" I muttered, before he evaporated into thin air.

"Did he just…did he…did…" Mel stuttered.

"No." I was even more confused. "We must have been seeing things. Let's go." I grabbed Mel with one hand and the door handle with the other, and in one fluid motion, opened the door, moved us inside, and closed the door behind us.

Smoke filled the air.

"What…the?" We coughed, choking on the thick cigar smoke that wafted up our nostrils and into our lungs.

"Hey kid, what are you doing here?"

Waving my hand in front of my face to clear the air around me, I peered into the room. "Who said that? Who are you? What are you doing in our room?"

Raucous laughter filtered through the haze, and my eyes focussed on the men sitting or standing around a table by the window.

"*Your* room?" one beefy guy at the table replied. He shuffled a pack of cards. "This ain't *your* room kid, it's the game room. We play cards and drink gin."

I recognised their type from old gangster movies. Wrinkled three-piece suits, fedora hats, and cigars permanently attached to their teeth. I waved away some smoke. "No, it's not. It's our room, room 23 at 2323 Old Beachside Way Motel."

More laughter.

"Nah, kid. It's the 23 battalion hideout, and we wanna know how you found it, and how'd you get in?" They all stood and straightened their clothes.

"Andy." Mel tugged on my sleeve. "I don't know what's happening, but I think we'd better get out of here."

I turned my head to her. "Why should we? It's *our* room."

"I don't think it is," she whispered as the men descended on us. She turned around, flung open the door, and dragged me into the hallway. The motel hallway with its red carpet and green walls. The door slammed shut behind us.

I coughed. "That was *our* room, Mel."

"But something's going on, Andy. I'm scared. That boy before, he's a ghost. That banging, why did it start and why did it stop? I'm scared."

I studied my sister's face. While we were a lot alike, we were so different. I was born fifteen minutes before her, but she matched my fearless antics at every step.

Until now.

"*Nothing is going on,*" I said, and stopped. The white-haired boy from before was back in the hall. But this time, he was a bit closer. "Who are you and what do you want?" I demanded of him. But, he just evaporated. Again.

This cannot be real! I almost stomped my foot in frustration. "Let's go, Mel, this is ridiculous. We must be having a bad dream." I dragged her into our room. But it wasn't our room. In fact, I wasn't sure if was even our world.

We stood on a desolate hill overlooking the ruins of a city before us, spreading across the horizon. Buildings were blown up, knocked down, and overgrown with weeds. The sky hung heavily with dark hues of blue, plumes of smoke rose in tendrils across the buildings, choking everything it came in contact with.

"Andy, what's that?"

Mel was pointing toward the sky. Or at least where the sky should be. An unearthly machine hovered there, with stalactites, made from God knows what, hanging from every inch of it.

We heard distant rumbling, and machinery crunching, and saw what we could not believe, huge robots walking amongst the leftovers of the city, thudding and thumping and crushing whatever was underfoot.

"Hey, kids, what you doin' out? You betta hide."

Mel and I turned as one toward the human sounding voice to see a man in filthy, torn clothes moving toward us.

"If they find you, they'll take you."

"Take us where?" I interrupted. "Where are we? What are they? Who are you?" I dazedly looked around. "What *is* this place?"

The man sniffed and wiped his nose on his sleeve as he stopped beside us. "What you mean, what is this place? Say…" He eyed us suspiciously. "Where you kids from? You're not from 'round 'ere. You're too clean." He picked at my pjs.

I shook him off. "*What is this place?*" I demanded with more bravado than I felt. "*Where are we?*"

"More importantly," Mel chimed in. "What *year* is it?"

I was surprised at her question. So was the man.

"What! You kids know nuffin'. It's the year 2323 an' this is, *was*, New York City."

"2323." I frowned.

"New York!" Mel gasped. "Oh, no, how awful."

The man became agitated. "Hey, here, those things have spotted us, you betta move if you wanna stay alive." He scurried off.

In the distance, we saw the mountainous mechanical men move toward us and we turned to flee, running smack bang into our door, which we flung open and fled through, landing right back in the hallway with its red carpet and green walls and flickering lights.

We spun around. There was no dilapidated NYC, no robotic monsters, just our door with the number 23 on it.

"I am so sick and tired of this," I said, getting to my feet. "*What is going on?*"

"Andy." She was pointing down the hall. Now, there were two white-haired boys standing in the hallway looking at us. They were our height, looked to be our age, both had bowl haircuts. The hairstyle itself was so old-fashioned, but their pyjamas mirrored our own.

"I'm done with this." I marched toward them ready for a confrontation, but once again they evaporated into thin air.

"Gutless cowards," I muttered. "This is rubbish." I walked back to Mel. "We need to go downstairs and find that old woman and demand to know what's going on."

"No, Andy, let's just go to bed. Come on, please," she pleaded, pulling me by my arm into our room.

"What's the point, we always end up…somewhere else…*where are we now?*"

We were standing on the porch of an old house looking toward the street. Oldsmobiles putted by, and people in old-fashioned clothes strolled down the street.

"Why, hello there," one man called out, tipping his hat in a welcome while the woman on his arm smiled and waved. "You must be new to the area. Welcome to Twenty-Third Street, Bakersville." He donned his hat and he and his waif-like wife tottered away in their old era clothes.

"Twenty-Third Street, Bakersville?" Mel tugged my sleeve. "Number 23 keeps popping up."

I turned around and saw the number on the front door. "It certainly does."

"Oh, my God," Mel gasped. "Number 23, Twenty-Third Street. 2323. The same as the motel we're staying at." She tugged my arm again. "What's happening must have something to do with the motel."

I sighed. "I don't know, but I'm sick and tired of it." With a defeated shrug I said, "come on," and opened the door to number 23.

And we were back in the hallway again.

"This is getting so old," I said. "I just want to go to bed and get some sleep. I'm so tired," I wailed, waving my hands in the air at an imaginary foe. But the foes were closer than I realised.

The two white-haired boys stood outside of our parents' door, standing in the middle of the hall, watching us as we watched them.

I stood there watching. I mean *really* watching. What was I going to do? They kept evaporating whenever I went near them, so they clearly weren't human. Or, I was clearly having a nightmare. Either way, there was no point fighting them. I have no idea how long we stood there in our face off, but Mel finally had enough.

"Come on, let's try again."

I let her pull me into our room and awaited our fate.

It was our room.

At least, it *looked* like our room, but it was bright and light and airy. We ran to the window and looked out. The sun was shining down upon the beach, and we saw people sunbaking and laughing and splashing in the ocean.

"No, Brutus, baby, you cannot go into the water. You'll die."

We glanced down to see a woman with a child pottering in the garden. She was planting the trees he handed to her, and he seemed awfully familiar, even if he was much younger.

"But, Mama." His lip quivered and drool dripped from his lips. "I want to go swimming with everyone else."

"No, Brutus," she snapped. "You cannot go swimming and I'm sick and tired of telling you. Now go and help the guests."

"That must be the old woman at the desk and that Brutus guy. But he's so young." Mel turned quizzically. "But he's not young now, so how long ago was that?"

I shrugged. "I dunno. But whatever this is, it needs to end. Let's go down and talk to that old woman." We made it out the door, but smacked head first into Brutus himself. The adult version that is.

"Where are you going?" he snivelled.

"Um, I, we, are going downstairs to talk to the woman at the desk."

"Sorry, she's in bed, and you should be too."

I noticed the two white bobbing things behind him and realised it was the twins we'd seen in the hallway.

"Sure, no problem." Mel pulled me backwards away from the drooling Brutus and schizoid twins. "Sure, we'll go back to bed. Not a problem. Good night." She pulled me through the doorway and slammed it shut on the gorilla and the bobbing twins.

I sighed, something I'd done a lot tonight. "This

is ridiculous!"

"What is?"

"Ah." We spun around to find ourselves at the front desk with the little old lady watching us.

"What is ridiculous?"

I had no idea what to say. My mouth opened to speak, but nothing came out.

"Something is seriously wrong here," Mel piped up. "We keep hearing noises, and seeing two white-haired boys in the hallway, and there's something wrong with our room."

"With your room?" she daintily inquired. "Well, let's see what room you're in, shall we." Running her finger down the registry book it stopped. "Oh, dear. Room number 23." She looked up. "Well, you do have bad luck, don't you?"

I cocked a brow and pursed my lips. "And why do you say that?"

"Why, dear." She trotted around from behind the desk. "Room 23 is haunted."

"Haunted?" Mel and I said together, me more in a 'this is ridiculous' kind of way, and her in a 'it can't possibly be true' kind of tone.

"Why, yes, dear," she started.

Was she growing? I wondered, seeing her become taller before our eyes.

The little old lady was a little old lady no more, taking up all of the space in the room. The voice deepened, the mouth widened, and five long sets of teeth, and two forked tongues pierced out into the air. "Room 23 is haunted."

The whole room was blood-red. My own blood pulsated wildly through my ears, the tongue lashed out.

"Ahhhh!" we cried together and raced for the stairs, up three flights, and along the hall to our room. The two white-haired boys were standing in the blood-red hallway pointing to our room.

"Ahhhh!"

We blew past them and into the room, slamming and bolting the door shut.

"I was wondering where you two were."

"Ahhhh!"

We jumped and spun around to see Mum unpacking our cases.

"You must've gone for a walk." She frowned. "The least you could have done was change into some clothes."

Mel and I looked down from our slumped positions against the door. Our pjs were tattered and covered in stuff. God knows what sort of stuff, but it was blood-red.

HE WHO OPENS THIS BOOK

"Hey Mickey, you ever been in that creepy old house on Fourteenth Street? You know, the one that looks a thousand years old?"

I chomped down on my meat pie and chewed, thinking about the question, and wondering why Billy Mendelson was standing in front of me in the lunch shed, asking me. I swallowed and took a sip of cola. "Nope! Why you askin'?"

"Well," he said eagerly, hopping from one foot to the other. "My brother and his mates went in yesterday, and they reckon that all the stories about it being haunted are rubbish. He said nothing happened, and dares everyone to go in there and prove him wrong."

I finished off my pie, screwed up the bag, and shot it into the bin like a basketball pro.

"Score!" Tim cried beside me and we high-fived.

"How many people you tellin' this to?" I asked Billy, finishing off my soda and sending the can after the bag. Score again!

"Everyone," Billy said. Turning around, he pointed

to the other kids. "I've told Lucas, Todd, Matt, Joe, Craig, Ben and Bobby." He turned back to me. "I'll tell everyone else later."

"Why are you telling people anyway?" Tim asked, standing and picking up his bag. "Why would we care what your brother does? He doesn't even go to this school."

The bell rang to end lunch and everyone started collecting their stuff.

"Exactly," I replied. "What does it matter what your brother does? Why are you tellin' everyone, and why's he daring us all?" We were walking toward our classroom when several other kids joined the conversation.

"Yeah," Lucas added. "I don't care to go to that old house. It doesn't interest me."

"Bet him and his mates lied anyway," Craig said, hefting his bag onto his shoulder. "Bet they didn't even *go* into the house. He's just lying about it to make himself look good and all big and brave."

"My brother *did* go in." Billy slammed his hands onto his hips and stood defiantly in front of everyone, almost daring us to say it again. "My brother is *not* a liar. He and his mates *did* go in and I know because I was there. I was taking pictures while they went in. So they *are not* liars. They *did* go in; *they did.*" Billy's eyes welled up, but he managed to keep the tears from falling.

"All right, Billy, all right." I glanced around at the others. "Your brother went into the old house on Fourteenth Street." I shrugged. "But that's got nothing to do with us." I noticed the freaked out expressions on everyone's faces as the last lunch bell rang.

Billy wiped his face. "Well," he muttered, "he's just daring everyone else to go in there and say it's not haunted."

I shrugged again. "Nothing to do with us, Billy." Tim and I left him at his classroom.

*****

"Have you thought about it?" Tim asked me after school. We were in my backyard playing with my German Sheppard, Rex, when the subject was brought up again.

"What?"

"Going into that old house on Fourteenth."

I threw the stick and Rex chased after it. "Why would I?"

"Aren't you the least bit curious?" Tim picked up the stick and waved it in front of Rex before throwing it.

I shrugged and put my hands on my hips. "Not really." Rex sat before me and dropped the bit of wood we were throwing. His big brown eyes implored me to throw it again. I mooshed his face and asked, "Who's a good boy, Rex?" before throwing it.

*****

The next day at school, everyone was talking about it. Billy had pretty much let every student know about his brother's dare, and now talk was spreading like wildfire about kids who were taking up the challenge.

"Maybe we should do it as a group or class?" Gary suggested between classes. We'd stopped in the hallway outside of the science room waiting for our teacher.

"I'm not interested," I told him. "It doesn't matter to me one way or the other about that old house."

More kids gathered in the hall.

"I think it would be awesome," Michelle added, twirling a braid. "I wouldn't want to go on my own though, I'd go in a group."

"So would I."

"Same here."

I sighed. Was this getting out of hand or what?

Mr Bourne raced up the hall. "Okay, kids, go in."

We piled in and took our seats as he spread papers on his bench.

"Okay," he addressed us. "Quieten down. Today we're going to talk about ghosts and the paranormal."

I glanced at Tim beside me. *What the?*

"Now, a lot of talk has gone around about the house on Fourteenth Street. And while I personally believe in science over the paranormal, I thought it would be a good idea to take a class trip to the house and find out for ourselves. How about it?"

How about what? What did he just say?

"Yeah!"

"That'd be awesome."

"Oh, it will be fun to go as a class."

All around me, my year ten science class moved with excitement at the proposal of a day trip to a supposed haunted house.

"Of course, I'll have to organise it and get permission slips signed. But, oh, what fun it will be."

*****

Ten days later, much to my disdain, we all stood outside of the house on Fourteenth Street. I'll try not to bore you with details, but it was an old Victorian two-storey wood house looking all ratty and tatty.

I could not believe we were here, giving into the speculation of ghosts that no one had ever seen. I lagged behind the group as we walked up the path and inside. I lagged behind from room to room and floor to floor, but was the first one outside for lunch which we ate on the grassy lawn out front. I also lagged behind when we went down to the basement. It was the last place of the day, and I couldn't wait to go home. I hefted my bag onto my shoulder and followed everyone down.

"Okay," Mr Bourne said, waving his arm around. "Let's see what's down here."

The basement wasn't huge, but it was empty. Not a stick of old furniture, no boxes, no toys, no nothing. The floor was pancaked dirt and dust flew through the air, stunned into existence by twenty-five school kids and their bat crap crazy science teacher traipsing through it.

I sneezed three times in a row, and got multiple

bless-yous. "Ah." I felt blocked when it was over, and circled after Tim as we went around the room.

"Well, kids, nothing to see here, so let's head out." Mr Bourne led us up the stairs.

"Yeah, well," I muttered. "I could have told you that." I waited my turn, and as I stepped forward, my foot caught on something and I face planted into the centuries-old dirt.

Tim turned around on the stairs. "You okay?"

"Ugh." I sneezed. "I tripped on something." I slowly crawled into a sitting position as Tim came down to help.

"What'd you trip on?" He aimed his flashlight around my feet.

"Dunno." I grabbed my bag out of the way and we saw something sticking out of the now loosened ground.

"What is that?" Tim moved the light closer. "Is that a book?"

We quickly brushed the dirt away and I pulled an old book out from its burial place.

"Whoa, how old is that?" Tim moved closer, putting his light directly over it so we could read the cover.

"*Mr Magarium's Old Book of Hilariums,*" I read and screwed my face up. "That doesn't even make sense, and there's no such word as hilariums."

"Open it up." Tim eagerly pawed at it, but no matter how hard we tried it wouldn't open.

Well, that could be because of the lock on the front!

"Guys, you coming?" Michelle yelled down the stairs.

I quickly shoved the book into my bag. "Coming." We clambered up the steps, through the house and into the afternoon sun.

"Are you all right, Mickey? You're a bit…" Mr Bourne pointed to my clothes.

I looked down to see I was covered in antique dust and dirt. "Ah, just tripped in the basement is all. I'm fine." I quickly patted myself down and most of the dust floated away. "Ugh, Mum's not going to like this." I looked at the reddish brown stains left behind.

*****

That night, she made me wash my own clothes before doing homework. Rummaging through my bag, I found it. The book. I stared at it. *Mr Magarium's Old Book of Hilariums*. The old gold lettering was faded, or missing altogether. There was no author name, and the old brown leather was worn from decades, if not centuries of use. The spine was tatty at both ends, and the paper looked to be quite yellow. But I wasn't going to know that until I opened it.

I pulled at the lock. It was old, rusted, and almost black with age. I should have been able to pull it apart or break it, considering how old it was, but I just couldn't budge it. I turned it over, running my fingers over the old leather. "How old are you?" I asked it, wondering if I could pick it. I got out my torch and held it over the lock. It was old and required an old-style key. *Don't have any of those lying around.*

"Mmm, what am I going to do with you?" I asked it. "How do I get you open?"

After much consideration, and Mum telling me to do my homework, I shoved the book onto a shelf in my bookcase and finished up for the night.

*****

"Hey," I said in surprise the next day at school. "How did you get in here?" I pulled the book out of my backpack.

"Hey, why didn't you tell me you'd brought it?" Tim said, reaching for it.

I pulled it away. "I didn't. I left it on my bookshelf last night. I didn't pack it."

"You must've if it's right here. Have you got it open yet?" Again, Tim reached for it, but again I pulled it away.

"Dude!" He was annoyed. "Let me look."

"It's just an old book," I said defensively, not wanting to hand it over. "What do you need to see it for?"

"Duh! Because we found it in an old so-called haunted house and I want to see it." Tim's expression showed bigger annoyance than his voice.

I reluctantly agreed and slowly handed it over.

He eagerly grabbed it and tried to open the lock.

"It won't open," I quickly jumped in. "I tried last night."

Tim examined it, turning it over and over. "Maybe I can get it to open."

"Doubt it." I reached for it. "Careful, it's old and I don't want you ruining it."

That stopped him. Wide-eyed he said, "Why would you care if I ruin it? It's just an old book and we found it in an old house."

I snatched it back. "Because," I snapped. "It *may be* an old book, but that doesn't mean you can wreck it. It *might* be valuable." I wrapped my jumper around it and put it back in my bag. "It needs to be treated with care."

"Dude." Tim frowned. "What's wrong with you? You're going nuts over an old book?" He softened. "But yeah, it could be valuable and we could sell it and make big bucks from it. Do you know how to open it?"

"Nope," I said, munching into an apple.

"It looks like it needs an old key. There's a locksmith in town, maybe he can help."

I thought about it. "Sounds like a good idea." With a nod of my head, I added, "I'll check into it on the weekend."

*****

I shoved the book back onto my shelf when I got home. "Maybe I put you in without realising?" I mumbled, and got on with my homework which I left unfinished when Mum called me down for dinner. When I got back upstairs, I noticed the book was sitting on my desk on top of my open English book.

"How did you...?" I scratched my head. "How did you...? I put you on the shelf, I know I did." And that's where I put it back and got on with my homework.

After packing my bag for the next day and getting ready for bed, I walked in to find the book sitting on my backpack that I'd left on the desk. I stopped short and looked around. Walking to the door I yelled downstairs. "Mum, were you in my room?"

"No," she yelled back. "Why?"

"Um, a book was moved is all."

"Maybe the cat knocked it over."

Yes, I thought, *Salem must have knocked it over.* I looked around for our jet-black cat that I'd named after the cat in *Sabrina the Teenage Witch* and found him sitting regally on the end of my bed balefully eyeing the book. "There you are, you rascal." I gave him a quick rub behind the ears and got a meow in return. "Did you knock my book off the shelf?" I held it up to him.

"Hisssss." His ears went back and a furry black paw swiped at the book.

"Hey." I yanked it away. "Careful."

Salem was back to normal and licking his paw.

I looked at the book. Maybe there was something weird about it. Why would Salem hiss at it? I held it out again and this time Salem screeched so loud Mum heard it downstairs. He bolted from the room and I heard Mum say, "what did you do to the cat?"

"Nothing," I called back. "Might've stepped on his foot or something…" My voice trailed off and I ducked back into my room and popped the book back on the shelf. "Now, you stay there," I told it with a shake of my finger.

*****

"Mmm…mmm…" I mumbled at being dragged from my sleep. I came to. My eyes slowly slid open to an unearthly green glow enveloping the room.

"Whah?" I blinked and rubbed my eyes. "Whah, whah's gooing on?" I yawned and sat up.

The book was hovering calmly in mid-air, in the middle of my room, surrounded by the eeriest green glow.

"*Mickey…Mickey…*"

"Whah? Whoo?"

"*Mickey…Mickey…*"

I flung the covers back and marched over to the book which was about chest height. I waved my arms above it, below it, around it. No strings, no wire, no joke. "Whah's going on?" I scratched my head and yawned again.

"*Mickey…Mickey…*"

Was the voice coming from the book? I grabbed it with both hands and pulled.

It resisted.

I pulled harder.

It pulled back.

I strained, pulling with all my might, digging my

heels into the carpet, straightening my backbone, and putting every ounce of everything I had into getting the book into my grasp.

The book stayed steadfast, and I ended up collapsing on the floor. I stared at it, floating in mid-air, surrounded by its green glow. The air felt chilly, cooler than normal, and now I noticed a musty old smell, probably emanating from the dirt engrained in the book.

"*Mickey...Mickey...*"

I watched as it swirled around the room, zigzagging, circling, weaving in patterns, finally coming to rest back on the shelf...

I woke up to morning light filtering into the room and jerked up to look at the book.

It was sitting on the shelf I'd placed it on the night before.

No!

It couldn't be!

That couldn't have been real?

I shook my head and got ready for school. I shook my head and had breakfast. I shook my head and grabbed my bag from my desk. I eyed the book on the shelf. It was still there. "And you're going to stay there," I told it and left for school.

"Cool, Mickey, you brought the book," Tim said after rooting around in my bag.

"What! No! I left it home." I spun around to see the book in Tim's hand. "How did...I left that...how did...?" It left me scratching my head in puzzlement.

"You know, I googled it last night. I found

nothing on Mr Magarium, or even the house on Fourteenth." Tim tugged at the lock. "Have you found a way of opening it yet?"

"Hey." I snatched at it. "Give it back."

"Hey, cool, what's that?" Billy called as he and a group of kids walked up to us.

"It's a cool old book we found in the basement of that creepy old house. Mickey tripped on it and we dug it up. How cool is it?" Tim held it up for all to see.

We found? "Give it back," I demanded and the guys turned to look at me. I held out my hand. *"Give it back!"*

"Nah, man." Tony grabbed it. "Let's have a look." He fumbled with the lock. "It doesn't open?"

"Nah, it doesn't, we tried it already and can't get it to open," Tim replied as the book was passed around.

"Hey," I yelled, making everyone stop. "Give it back," I demanded through clenched teeth. I grabbed at it, but the idiots I was with started passing it around faster.

"It's not a game of pass the parcel," I said. "Give it here." I was mad they were playing stupid games with an old book that was possibly priceless.

It was passed around from kid to kid, all prying, digging, ripping at the lock.

"Stop it, you'll wreck it."

"Hey, let's take it to the tech shed and see if we can open it," Tim yelled and they took off running.

"Hey." I grabbed my bag and ran after them, finding them attacking the book with screwdrivers and hammers.

"What the hell's wrong with you lot?" I slammed the door behind me. Everyone stopped and turned. "It's an old book, it could be valuable and worth something, but not if you lot wreck it." They guiltily looked from me to the book back to me.

"Besides," I added. "I found it, so it's mine. I didn't tell you lot you could play with it." I moved forward to take it.

Gary whipped his arm up and back, still holding the book. "You found it in the house, so technically it's not yours." He held up his other hand to stop me. "It belongs to whoever owns the house."

"No one owns the house," Tim said. "I googled last night. All relatives are dead; there's no living owner."

We all looked at him. "Well, then," I said smugly. "It's mine because I found it. Give it." I held out my hand with a cocky look and raised brow.

"We should at least try and open it." Gary reluctantly, slowly, lowered his arm. "We'll be careful."

I shook my head. "I don't know."

Todd brandished a screwdriver. "Don't you want to know what's in it? I do."

"I dunno." I shook my head. Did I? Didn't I? I wasn't sure after last night. Did I imagine that or what? "Look, just give it back and I'll think about it." I reached for it and Gary turned and ran. Chasing him around the tech shed, much to my annoyance and everyone else's cheers, I managed to grab him. We lurched into a counter and I got my hand on the book and yanked. As we fell against the sink next to us, my elbow hit the large handle that stuck out into the middle. It moved to the side, turning it on, and splashing water onto the book.

"Hey, you got it wet," I yelled, quickly wiping my sleeve over it.

"Hey, it's smoking!" Todd said, pointing to my hands.

The book started vibrating, moving, shaking, smoke twirling up in tendrils. It shook from my hands to float in the air.

"Whoa," everyone said in unison.

We stood around the book in awe, watching it whirl and twirl and dance around in circles.

The book burst open and pages flapped wildly before remaining open at one page in particular. The book floated down to waist height and we circled it.

"He who opens this book will forever be cast within it," I read.

"What does that mean?" Tim muttered beside me.

Smoke rose, the green glow grew, and all of a sudden I was sucked like a leaf in a frenzied tornado into the book.

"Whoa," Tim said. "Mickey? Mickey?"

*****

On Fourteenth Street, in the basement of the creepy old house, a book called *Mr Magarium's Old Book of Hilariums* fell into the hole it had been dug up from.

Dirt moved to cover it, bury it, remove it from

history until the next time it was ready to be unearthed by a boy, or girl, whose fate was to trip on it.

THE HAUNTING OF TIKI ISLAND

"Oh, my God, this is going to be so cool." Elsa, my older sister, clapped her hands together in excitement.

I went from watching her to looking across the stern of our boat; a huge cruise ship making its way to Tiki Island. We would be staying there for a whole week, and so far, I didn't like the look of it one bit. I walked over to my twin brother, Mark. "What do you think?"

"Of what?" Identical blue eyes looked into mine.

"This island!" I nodded towards the small South Pacific island we were nearing. The beach and palm trees were in view, and there was some sort of red banner strung between two large tree stumps…or something.

"I reckon it's cool," Mark replied, holding up his binoculars to scope out our holiday destination. "I can't wait to climb the volcano and see what's inside."

Um, yeah. Forgot to mention that, didn't I. Yep, there's a volcano on the island. Hasn't gone off in hundreds of years apparently, and we've been told it doesn't plan to go off anytime soon, so we were perfectly safe.

I eyed it. It did look pretty awesome, and there were old lava tubes we could explore. Or so I had read in the brochure.

"Ooohhh look, big massive tikis are holding the welcome banner up."

I grabbed the binoculars and peered through. "God, how long did they take to carve?"

"Dunno, but how cool are they?" Mark snatched the binocs back.

I continued watching the island get bigger and bigger as we sailed into the small harbour and pulled alongside the dock. Our bags had already been packed, so we met our parents on the deck and finally made our way down the gangplank, along the dock, and up to the huge red banner that read "Welcome to Tiki Island". The two tikis that held it up towered above our heads so high we craned our necks just to try and see the tops of them.

"Welcome to Tiki Island," boomed through a microphone and we all saw a huge bulky man in a three-piece white suit standing on a small stage under the banner.

"I am Mr Magoo, how do you do?" He doffed his hat and we saw the big balding head underneath.

Mark nudged me and I saw the excited expression on his face, and Elsa was clapping her hands and doing a little jig in place. I looked back at Mr Magoo.

"I am the owner of Tiki Island, and I cannot wait

for you all to holiday here. I hope you enjoy your stay, and that you'll all join me for dinner at 6 p.m."

I glanced at my watch. It was already four.

"Without further ado, it was nice to meet you, and please take a buggy up to the motel."

I wiped my face on my t-shirt sleeve and yanked off my cap. It was hot standing in the summer sun, and I was grateful we were moving at a quick pace.

Staff loaded passenger's luggage onto carts attached to golf buggies on which the guests were hitching a ride. We loaded up ours and went whizzing toward the huge eight-storey white building spread across the island. Each floor was back from the one below so it looked like a layered cake. The volcano rose behind the building and palm trees surrounded the front.

As we unloaded at the front door, I saw pools with slides off each side of the entrance and brightly coloured birds flapped around bird feeders hanging from all of the trees.

We three kids were sharing one room while our parents had the one adjoining.

"Why don't you kids change into your swimmers and go spend an hour in the pool?" Mum called through the open doorway. "I'll unpack your stuff."

"Cool," we said in quick succession and pulled off our clothes to change. We got downstairs as fast as we could, raced for the pool, and dive bombed into the deep end.

Coming up for air, I trod water while looking around. The slide was carved with tikis, and small gardens and palm trees surrounded the slide and pool. Other kids were splashing around and yelling and screaming and more were coming to join us.

I saw Mark head for the slide and waited to see him come out.

"Woohoo," he screamed, waving his arms in the air as he shot out of the tube's opening and into the pool. He surfaced and found me. "Oh, my God, Danny, come and do it. You gotta do it."

I swam over and joined him, and before we knew it, fun time was over and we had to head back upstairs.

"Have quick showers and get dressed." Mum was bustling around our room. "I'm laying out your clothes as dinner's in half an hour, so make it quick."

I turned for the bathroom, but Elsa was shutting the door behind her.

"Make it quick," Mum called through the door.

Except quick to Mum is completely different to Elsa. She came out after fifteen minutes and then Mark beat me to it. I sighed and sat back on my balcony chair and watched the surroundings going on below.

Staff scurried around like worker ants, and some kids were still in the pools. The cruise ship bobbed quietly at the dock, and the sun was slowly moving for the horizon.

"Done," Mark yelled.

I made my way into the bathroom and was out in five minutes, and we were seated at our table in the grand dining room at six on the dot.

"Oooh, lobster." Mum read the menu. "I wonder if I should splurge?"

"It's already paid for," Dad said. "It's all inclusive of the price."

"Does that mean *we* can have lobster?" Elsa's eyes sparkled at the proposal of having such a meal for the first time ever. In fact, it would be a first time for any of us kids.

"Sure." Dad put his menu away. "As long as you eat it and don't waste any."

The waiter took our orders, served us chilled drinks in tiki-shaped glasses, and finally brought out steaming plates of food.

I'd gone with chowder, but eyed off Mark's steak, and the lobster Mum, Dad and Elsa had in front of them.

After the main meal was eaten Mr Magoo got up to speak. "Ladies and gentlemen and bald headed babies with their hair parted on the side." He doffed his white Panama hat with a twinkle in his eye. "Thank you for joining us here on Tiki Island. We have much in store for you all. Fun and games and crazy days, including…" he whipped something small out of his pocket, "the tiki hunt."

"Hunt?" Mark perked up. "I love a good hunt."

"That's right," Magoo went on as I glanced around the room. "On this island there are one hundred tiki idols like this." He waved the small thing in the air. "You can try and find them. At the end of each day you can trade them in for special prizes, and," he waved his arm at the captive audience, "at the end of the week, whoever has collected the most tikis, will get a very special prize indeed."

"What is it?" an excited boy yelled from a table in front of the stage.

Magoo moved closer. "Ah," he said to the boy, "*that* is a surprise. So," he moved on, "starting from tomorrow, feel free to run and search, but don't worry parents, they will be perfectly safe as we have child-proofed the whole island," he winked, "even the volcano."

Nervous laughter filtered through the room and Magoo left the stage. Turning back to our plates, we saw dessert had been laid before us. A huge volcano was spewing red-orange lava at us.

"Whoa, look at that." Mark poked it and it bubbled over the side and poured down onto the plate. "How cool is that?"

I poked mine and let the lava flow over my finger. I sucked it off. "Sherbety fizzy bombs," I said and shoved my fork into the chocolate mud cake.

"Oh, my God, this is so good," Elsa mumbled around a mouthful of cake, her eyes moving to the heavens before closing.

"Don't talk with your mouth full," Mum admonished before shoving in a forkful. "Mmm, mmm." Her eyes closed against the chocolatey goodness.

After dinner, we watched the fireworks from our balcony then got ready for bed.

"Hey Danny, you wanna get your own tikis or join up and share whatever the prizes are?" Mark flung his bed covers back and jumped in.

I pulled on my t-shirt. "I suppose we could join up then we'd both win, or," I pulled a wicked grin and jumped into my own bed, "I could get all the tikis and claim the prize for myself."

He threw a pillow at me. "You would *so* lose," he said with an eye roll.

I threw the pillow back. "Would *so* not," I replied.

*****

I'm not sure what woke me up. It could have been Elsa's murmuring, or Mark's snoring, or it could have been sleeping on solid ground after a week of being on a boat. But something did.

I blinked a few times, got rid of the blurriness, and saw a soft yellow glow coming through the open balcony doors. I quietly sneaked over to the billowing curtains and peeked out. I saw lots of little yellow things floating around. Wait, what are they?

Stepping onto the balcony, I strained for the slightest sound. Voices mumbled, hummed. *Those must be the fire torches,* I thought. *But why are so many people out with torches at this time of night?* I watched the lights spread up the pathways and eventually disappear into the woods. This was *too* weird not to investigate.

I woke Mark up and covered his mouth. "Get dressed," I whispered. "We're going out." He silently nodded and we threw on our clothes from dinner.

Sneaking out of our room and down the corridor, we decided to take the stairs instead of the lift so no one would know we were coming. Flight after flight we found no one. Into the lobby, we ducked behind a massive wood tiki and found no one. It was deserted.

I frowned and beckoned Mark toward the open front door. We silently raced outside and hid behind another tiki because, well, they were all over the place. The main entrance was empty, like no one else was on the island.

I nudged Mark along the path I'd seen the torches float along and flicked on my torch that I'd brought with us.

"What are we doing?" Mark whispered in my ear.

"Checking something," I whispered back and pulled him down the path. It wound and turned, we ducked and dived, and finally caught glimpses of glowing light between the branches.

We made our way to the edge of a small hill before I yanked Mark behind a tree.

Two people walked past us carrying their burning torches.

"It cannot be," one said. "I really do not want to be here anymore. All of these things happening."

Our heads turned in their direction and we strained to hear the rest of it, but didn't catch any more. Once we were sure they were gone, we stepped out, made it to the top of the hill, and stopped.

"Whoa," came out of us.

The volcano was on fire.

*****

We waited until after breakfast the next morning when we'd started our tiki hunt before talking about the night before.

"I wonder what made it glow." Mark pulled up stones along the path.

"Make sure you put those back," I said and stuck my hand into the hollow of a fake tree. I grabbed and pulled. "Got one," I yelled before Mark shushed me.

"We don't want people to know," he said, and looked at the tiki in my hand.

"Number 88," I read from the bottom. "Cool." I zipped it into the bag I had around my neck. "As for the volcano," I added quietly. "Maybe it's still active and they're not telling us." We continued our search along the path. "It could have been lava. It was glowing from the top and orange stuff was coming down the sides."

"Then wouldn't it be dangerous for us to be here?" Mark tried some tree holes and moved a couple of logs. "If it's an active volcano we're in danger."

We found ourselves back on the hillside looking up at the volcano. It looked dormant, and there was no glow or rivers of lava now. We glanced at each other and made the silent decision to go on. Following the trail, as narrow as it was, we eventually came to a tunnel buried deep in the undergrowth.

"This must be an old lava tube." I pulled on the vines and made a hole big enough for us to duck through. I swung my torch around, marvelling at the smoothness of the rock.

"This is cool," Mark whispered and we moved on.

The tunnel wound and weaved, and who knew how many there were, or where they led, but we descended then ascended, and finally emerged into a rather hot room that had red hot lava running through it.

"Whoa, this is hot." I waved the air in front of my face. "It's like a sauna."

"Or a volcano belly." Mark took a few steps toward the flowing river of red and orange heat slowly meandering on its way past us.

"If this were real, wouldn't it be hotter and wouldn't we be dead from the heat and fumes?" I asked as I searched the cavern.

"True," Mark replied. "So while it may be hot, make that very hot, I don't think this is real. Remember, Magoo said the island had been child-proofed, including the volcano. So this can't be real." He bent down and held his hand over the lava. "Not very hot." He lowered his hand until it was nearly touching it. "Not very hot at all."

"Careful," I admonished, sounding like Mum, and making an inspection of the walls. "Ah, steam ducts." I got a burst in the face. "Ouch, hot." I saw Mark smell his hand. "What *are* you doing?"

He looked up. "I don't know what this is, but it ain't lava. Just pretend." He stood up and dusted himself off. "Let's keep—"

"Whoa!"

The ground shook and we stuck our arms out to

keep our balance.

"Are we having an earthquake?" I yelled, trying to stay on my feet.

"Or a volcano quake?" Mark said as the rumbling died down.

We gasped for breath, but found it hard in the steamy air. "Let's get out of here," we yelled and bolted for the tunnel.

The ground shook again as we burst through the vines and raced back up the path, but instead of returning to the front of the motel, we somehow found ourselves at the back and ducked into the bushes as some of the staff came outside.

"Did you feel it, that rumble? Mr Magoo says island is not haunted. Island is not real volcano. But he says nothing about the rumbling. We must have earthquake and he just doesn't care."

We saw them sit at a table, cigarettes in hand.

"I have had enough," another said. "Night after night, things go missing, or are misplaced, and staff get blame, but Magoo says Tiki ghosts just having fun. We are called thieves even though we did not steal, and now, we must run around island every night after some ghost. Did you see volcano was on fire last night? What is doing that?"

"I've been here since the first day," a third man said. "I am the only original staff member left; all the others have been fired or quit because they think island is haunted—"

"Haunted by what?"

"By spirits of tikis," he continued. "They say they

see tikis floating down hallways and paths and through motel. They say tikis even set that fire last month. They say island is haunted and visitors have even gone missing."

I swear I heard a freight train coming, but realised that was the rumbling of an earthquake. Mark and I held onto each other and the tree in front of us. A few of the staff screamed. "There it is. If the volcano is not real then why is it shaking? Ah, look."

We followed his pointing finger up toward the volcano and saw lava flowing down the sides and spitting from the top.

"Cripes!" I muttered and we took off at a marathon pace back to the motel where we found guests flooding out the door and heading for the ship. There were mad screams and wails as parents called for their children.

"Ladies and gentleman," boomed over the loudspeaker. "This is *not* an earthquake, and the volcano is not on fire. It is purely part of the adventure of Tiki Island."

People stopped and quietened down, and our parents found us. Elsa trailed after them.

"Ladies and gentleman, the *volcano* is a fake. The *lava* is fake. The island moved to make you feel you are staying with an actual volcano. It's all part of the show. Please, you are not in any danger, please return to what you were doing and continue having fun. Please. Thank you ladies and gentleman."

Everyone was looking around, with dazed, surprised, or scared expressions on their faces. Mark and I exchanged a look. We knew what we would be doing later tonight.

*****

We spent the rest of the day looking for idols, and before dinner cashed them in for souvenirs, t-shirts and stationery items like pens and erasers.

Mark threw his pack on the bed. "That was a waste just for rubbish."

I held up the t-shirt and studied the design on the front. A huge tiki in the middle of an island with a little motel and volcano. "I know." I stuffed my pack into my bag. "If the gifts are this bad, imagine what the grand prize is."

*****

Once everyone had gone to bed, we waited until two o'clock to sneak out. Once again, there was no one around. Everything was empty. The halls, staircase, lobby. We sneaked along the path to the volcano and found it glowing like the night before. It looked real enough, for anyone who didn't know any better, they probably wouldn't be able to tell.

We scrambled through the bushes into the entrance, and followed the tunnel back to the lava room. The place was deserted, and we looked for another way out. No luck. It was a choice of the tunnel we'd come through, or the tunnel the lava was floating through.

I bent down over the river to look down the tunnel, but couldn't see much.

"Danny." Mark's voice was barely a whisper.

I looked up. "What?"

Mark was pointing to five huge wooden tikis floating in front of us.

"What the!" I stood beside him and aimed my torch at them. They hovered closer, circling us, trapping us against the river.

"Help us…" whispered through the steamy air. "Help us…"

I took a step back and stumbled. Righting myself, I swung my torch at them. "Stay back." Sweat poured down my face. "Stay back."

They came closer, floating in the air. How did they do that? They couldn't be real? It must be the steam causing us to hallucinate.

Mark lashed out at one, but it was unfazed by its encounter. "D-Danny," he stuttered. "What's going on? They can't be real."

"You wouldn't think so, would you?" I noticed they had cut off our escape by floating side by side and pushing us back toward the river, which seemed to be the only route left to take.

"Mark, I think we're going to have to…Mark…"

"Ah." He floundered, tumbling backwards into the lava. The tikis moved for me and I stumbled, felt myself fall, and was enveloped by the flow.

Have I died?

Am I drowning?

I surfaced and choked for air. Flinging the warm

red goop from my hand, I wiped my face and saw Mark a few feet ahead of me. I swam to him, and together we floated down the river of orange-red jelly-like substance that was definitely *not* lava.

We floated into a wide cavern filled with boxes, and managed to grab hold of a rocky outcrop and pull ourselves up and out of the goop. Panting, we lay behind some boxes and wiped off as much as possible.

"Ugh, what is this?" I groaned. "It stinks."

"Some sort of gel solution, I think," Mark said, wiping it from his hair.

I finished cleaning myself as best I could and looked around at the boxes. "Wonder what's in these." I lifted a lid and found bars of shiny gold. "No, these can't be," I muttered.

"What?" Mark stood beside me. "Is that gold?" He picked up a bar. "It's heavy like real gold."

It sat shining in the glow from the fire torches and raging fake lava river.

"Hey!" We were grabbed by the scruff of our necks.

"What are you two doing in here?" the gruff voice asked in our ears as the man hauled us along a tunnel and into a well-lit cavern where he threw us on the ground.

"Well, well, well."

We looked up to see Magoo and the ship's captain, plus twenty or so staff members from the motel and ship.

"What are we going to do with you two?"

ABOUT THE AUTHOR

T.K. is a children's TV show veteran who loves watching disaster and creature/zombie movies and TV shows, but not at night.

T.K. started writing many a year ago back in primary school, but only started her author career in 2015 with the release of her first three stories and anthology. She will write and release stories until there are twelve *Bones* books and a special edition numbered 13…

T.K. lives in Australia, loves extra cheesy cheeseburgers and chocolate, and gets a kick out of watching funny dog and cat videos.

T.K. Wrathbone is the kid's/tween pen name for author Tiara King. You can find more about Tiara on her website; follow her on social media, or visit her publishing house, Royal Star Publishing.

SOCIALS

tkwrathbone.com

tiaraking.com.au

royalstarpublishing.com.au

Sign up for *Tiara's* Newsletter…

Make sure you're always in the know and never miss free exclusives, the latest news, book updates, and so much more with newsletters from…

tiaraking.com.au

HAVE YOU READ THESE?

Next Top Mannequin
Cinderfella and Princess Charming: Witch Hunters
www.badluck-youredead.com
The Bones of Wrath: Changes
One Bone: Anthology 1

The Orphanage
Hantel and Gresel: Food Critics
Mirror, Mirror On The Wall
The Bones of Wrath: Haunted
Two Bone: Anthology 2

The Howler
Shadow Walkers
Faded
The Bones of Wrath: Ghosts
Three Bone: Anthology 3

I Spy With My Little Eye
Knock, Knock…Who's Dead?
It Creeped At Midnight
The Bones of Wrath: Monsters
Four: Anthology 4

OR THESE?

Trick Or Treat
All Hallows Possession
They Rise On A Blood Moon
The Bones of Wrath: Horrors
Five Bone: Anthology 5

All Clowns Must Die!
The Demon Resides
Infestation
The Bones of Wrath: Terrors
Six Bone: Anthology 6